LAST
OF THE
TIMEKEEPER

DAMIEN BUCKLEY

Last Moon of the Timekeeper
A Rybban Archive Novella

By

Damien Buckley

I

Time can be a fascinating concept, if you are fortunate enough to understand its complexity, which, Cregg found, most people did not. *He* understood time. Time was the most important part of his life, yet for almost everyone else he knew, time was nothing more than something to be wasted. Squandered, even. Time was precious, and there was never enough of it. If time was a commodity to keep, then Cregg was its guardian. Aside from himself, the only other who understood its true nature was Amser, the Architect of Time. Cregg had never met him, though he would very much like to. If there was anyone else on Rybban who would appreciate a life's work dedicated to the understanding of time—in all its forms and intricacies—it would be Amser.

Cregg tapped at a long glass tube and nodded as the sand trickled through its centre. The tube was one of many, laid out in an intricate formation around a tall stone pillar on the ground floor of his tower. He had designed it—with expert precision—himself, and had cost him much more than the time it measured. He paid for his labour with years of his life, and the final years with his wife, too. Had it all been worth it? If he let himself believe it wasn't, then what was the point of it all? Cregg made himself believe that his life's work, laid out in all its perfection on that pillar, was justified. Otherwise, well, he couldn't bring himself to think about that.

As the individual grains of sand filed through the tiny aperture and reached their marker, Cregg compared them to another smaller invention of his. One he carried by hand, three times a day to the top of the Moonwatch Tower. For fifty years he'd lived in the tower as both custodian and keeper of time in a small residence one hundred and eighty-seven steps below the bell chamber at the top. He knew every step. All were the same, yet each one unique, worn by thousands upon thousands of daily footsteps, up and down. One hundred and eighty-seven steps. Each one now torture on his hips and knees, as he too wore out with age. A long life of endurance, precision, and dedication. All in the name of time.

One hundred and eighty-seven.

The moment the sand reached the exact marker on the glass, determined by years of experimentation, he inverted the instrument in his hand. It was a simple design. Functional, and constructed only for his use. Two small glass bulbs, connected at the centre by only the narrowest of openings, holding a precise quantity of golden sand. A plain metal frame surrounded the glass—two flat plates with three thin rods holding it all together. He called it a *timer.* He had designed it himself and was proud of it. Not that he'd shown it to anyone else, except his wife, Petral. She had, of course, been indifferent, as she was with all his inventions.

'I will never understand this obsession of yours,' she would say, often, 'but if it makes you happy.'

That was it, though. It didn't make him happy. Happy was the wrong word. Satisfied, yes, certainly. His work gave him a sense of purpose he'd found nowhere else in his life. Happiness? Not for a long time.

One hundred and eighty-seven steps. The timer's sole purpose was to measure the time it took him to climb all of them. One at a time, one foot after the other. From the moment he turned it, he had until the last grain of sand touched the bottom to reach the top of the tower. It was important. Vital.

Lately, he'd noticed the sand running out faster, with more and more steps left to climb before he reached the top. Time and age were catching up with him. It wasn't the sand moving faster, it was *him* slowing down. He'd considered adjusting his wall instrument—his calendar—to allow himself longer to reach the top of the tower. That would mean admitting there would come a point when he'd no longer be able to fulfil his duty. Stubbornly, he pushed his joints to their limits, to reach the top before the sand in his timer expired.

One hundred and eighty-bloody-seven.

Out of breath, and at the summit of the tower, he looked west out across the city. The burnt orange sky looked empty without a cloud in sight. It had been too long without rain now, and a thin layer of dust hung in the air that blurred the horizon. He could still see, though, the faint pink tinge where land met the sky. A new day was beginning—an important day—and the moon would grace the world with her presence as she always did, right on time.

Cregg set his timer on the waist-high balcony shelf and

watched the dusty sky through the glass as the last remnants of time in the upper bulb joined the rest in the bottom. It was time. As the sand stopped falling, the first hint of the moon appeared as a thin line on the edge of the sky. He picked up an oversized metal hammer from its proper place by the wall, hefting it with both hands. It, too, felt heavier the older he became. He raised the hammer high and struck —only once—the giant bronze bell suspended from the ceiling in front of him. He winced, as he always did, as the chime of metal on metal vibrated through him and out across the city. It was a new day. It was Last Moon Day. A day of hope and celebration. A day of endings and new beginnings.

The ringing continued in his ears long after the bell itself had fallen silent. It was almost permanent now, after fifty years of striking the bell three times a day, every day, without omission. Through illness and injury, even on the day Petral died, he climbed those steps and did his duty. The tower, the bell and the hammer. Time. He knew little else in this life.

On the far side of the tower came a rustling sound. Quiet and hidden. Cregg smiled to himself and carefully replaced the hammer against the wall in its proper place. He reached into his pocket and retrieved a small cloth wrap before walking around the bell to the source of the noise.

'Still alive then,' he said, as he began unwrapping the piece of cloth.

From within a crevice between two old and weathered stone bricks in the tower wall, the head of a dragon appeared, regarding Cregg with black, unblinking eyes. The dragon hesitated for a moment before it carefully and clumsily exited the crevice and pulled itself up the stonework.

Once it reached the top of the wall in the opening, looking east toward the unseen sun, the dragon settled, already exhausted.

Cregg tutted quietly. 'Age gets to us all in the end,' he said to the dragon. 'You and I are not so different in that.' Within the unravelled cloth were two slivers of dried meat. He tore off the end of one, a piece no larger than his fingernail, and offered it to the creature as it flapped its long, slender tail back and forth, brushing away the dust that had settled there.

The dragon cocked its head, eyeing up the meal on offer. It sniffed at the meat before gingerly taking it in its mouth. The animal was barely bigger than Cregg's fist, and had one winged forearm missing, along with several scales along both sides of its dark red body. It was old and broken, but still had enough fight within it to cling on to life. As Cregg watched it chew on the meat, he wondered what it would be like to be a dragon.

They were hated creatures. Feared, and not without good reason. For centuries, they had been a blight on the lives of everyone. Dragon swarms regularly destroyed crops and buildings with the fiery liquid they spat. Not this one, though. It was too old—too injured—to be a threat to anything or anyone. It couldn't fly, and its spit was barely more than a dribble. Cregg had found it on its back, on the top step of the tower five days ago. The right thing would have been to crush it under his boot. Against his better judgement, he'd taken pity on the dragon, and gave it water and scraps of food.

Cregg wondered why he'd spared this one's life. It wasn't the first dragon he'd found within the tower, and it wasn't even the first one with an injury. Now, five days after finding it, he didn't know what else to do with it, other than bring it food. The dragon would never survive on its own, not that anyone would agree that it should. Nor could he bring himself to put it down. If he ever got caught with it, he would likely spend his final days languishing in prison for the crime of endangering others. That was unlikely, though, as no other soul had come to the top of the tower in over a decade.

Harmless in old age, the dragon was safe to live out however long it had left, hidden in a crevice where nobody else would know. Even so, Cregg felt the guilt gnaw away at his conscience. In all his life, only once had he ever broken the law, back when he was a boy and didn't know better. He offered the dragon more meat, his own stomach rumbling at the smell.

'If Petral were still alive, and she found out you were here, she'd kill me herself.'

The dragon stared at him, chewing. It didn't understand.

'Well, she's not here, so I suppose we're both off the hook. No idea what I'm supposed to do with you, though.' He held out the remaining scrap of meat, but the dragon refused it, pushing it away with its snout.

'Had enough, have you? Well, I'll leave it here in case you change your mind.' He placed the scrap on the wall beside the dragon, scrunched up the cloth, and pocketed it. 'Time for me to go. Don't go telling anyone our little secret now, will you?'

The dragon turned on the spot and settled down on the wall, curled up with its tail wrapped around its weary body. As old and beaten as it looked, Cregg swore he could see gratitude in its eyes.

One hundred and eighty-seven steps were easier to

manage when going down them rather than up. That is, until he'd descended forty-three of them, when he realised he'd left his timer at the top. In all his years, this was the first time he'd forgotten it. Cursing to himself, he counted his way to the top, tutted at the now sleeping dragon—as if it was to blame—and collected his timer. In his haste to grab the device, a loose piece of stone wall broke away, falling to the ground below. He cursed to himself, hoping it didn't hit a poor unsuspecting soul passing by. The tower was ancient— one of the first structures built in the city, and it, too, was fraying at the edges of age. Many times he'd requested repairs from the palace, and for years those requests were unanswered. The city was poorer now than he'd ever known it to be.

To make up for lost time, he hurried back down the steps. He made it all the way to one hundred and sixty before his left knee twinged and gave out. The final twenty-seven steps went by in a painful blur. His timer trailed behind him, having lost his grip on it. On the third step from last, the timer shattered, scattering sand and splinters of glass in all directions. Time was lost in more ways than one, as Cregg lay on his back at the bottom of the steps, groaning in pain.

2

Old age prevented him from getting up right away. Long gone were the days when a trip or fall could be brushed away as if nothing had happened. He ached enough on a *good* day. This was already far from a good day. He turned his head to the left and watched as the sand trickled the seconds away in his time measuring contraption. He contemplated its design as he lay there, witnessing time slip away. Like the sand, time only flowed in one direction. *Oh, how wonderful it would be to control time. To be the Architect of Time; Amser. He could make time flow backwards, surely? Let me be with Petral again.*

Then, something caught his eye.

In a dark corner behind his invention, he swore he saw something move. *Another dragon?* He lifted his head for a better look, a move he instantly regretted, such was the pain. The something in the shadows moved again, and it was too large to be a dragon.

'Who goes there?' he demanded, mustering up all he could to make his voice sound threatening and authoritative.

No reply came. The shadow still moved, barely, as if who or whatever was behind the calendar was trying too hard to keep still.

'I know you're there, so you may as well give yourself up and come out before you break something.' He tried again to sit himself up, without success.

Slowly, a mop of blond hair emerged, followed by a pair of timid eyes. 'Am sorry, sir,' came a voice, quietly.

'Sorry for what? Breaking in?' Cregg turned his head away from the boy to look at the door. The only door. It was closed and undamaged. He looked back at the boy. 'How *did* you get in?'

'Mean no harm to ya, sir. I simply needed somewhere to hide for a little while. Until it was safe again.' The boy remained partially hidden behind the pillar, apparently unwilling to reveal himself entirely.

'Safe? From whom?'

The boy didn't answer.

'Well, if you're not going to tell me anything, the least you can do is help me to my feet.'

The boy didn't move at first. Tentatively, and after what seemed like a day, the boy stepped out from the shadows. Likely no older than fourteen, he wore dirty clothes that were too big for him, and looked malnourished. Cregg figured him to be a street thief until he noticed a copper band on his wrist. *A slave.*

'Come on then, I can't be lying here all day. Help me up.' He reached out a hand to the boy, his shoulder complaining with pain.

The boy hesitated, but eventually edged across the hallway. He took Cregg's outstretched hand in his, and pulled. It was painfully clear the lad had no strength to him at all, though the assistance was enough for Cregg to get to his knees before heaving himself upright. When all was said and done, and aside from a few bruises and injured pride, the fall hadn't done too much damage.

'Thank you,' said Cregg. 'Now, tell me what you're doing here. This tower isn't open to the public.'

The boy took a step backwards, with a guilty look all over his face, as he withdrew into himself. He didn't speak.

'My name is Cregg. I am the timekeeper here. What do they call you? I assume you *do* have a name?' He offered a smile, trying to appear as friendly and as unthreatening as he could.

'Milo,' the boy said eventually, still looking guilty, as if ashamed of his own name.

'Ah, now that's better, isn't it? Well, Milo, as I say, you shouldn't be in here. Perhaps it is time you were on your way and we'll say no more about it, eh?'

Milo didn't move. He stared at Cregg with wide blue eyes, one of which was turned in towards his nose. Somewhere outside came a crash, followed by someone shouting. Whatever was going on outside startled Milo, and he withdrew farther back towards his hiding place. The commotion outside wasn't of any concern to Cregg, but Milo was obviously too terrified to leave.

'Please stay away from that. It's very delicate,' Cregg said. He'd already seen his timer shattered today, and couldn't bear it if anything happened to his life's work.

'What is it?' That one simple question indicated a shift in the boy. In an instant, Milo had gone from terrified child to inquisitive visitor. He stood in front of the pillar of stone and glass, and moved his head in a circle, taking in the sight of it all.

'I call it a calendar,' said Cregg, taking a step closer to the boy, who now had his back to him, his guard dropped.

'What's it for?'

'I use it to keep track of time. I built it myself. It took most of my life to make it accurate.' He couldn't hide the pride in his voice.

'Why do ya need to keep track of time? Do ya think ya might lose it?'

Cregg chuckled. 'No, not exactly. Let me show you. You see how the sand in the tubes moves at different speeds? This one on the left, it's much slower than this one here on the right.'

Milo shrugged. 'I guess.'

'This one,' Cregg pointed at the large cylinder of glass on the left. 'This measures a year. The one next to it measures a month and is fourteen times faster than that one. Then we have days. Thirty-three days in a month. And then these cylinders tell me the days, then hours and minutes.'

'Why?' asked Milo, furrowing his brow, trying to understand.

'Why what?'

'What's it for?'

'I already told you. It keeps track of time.'

'Why?'

The back of Cregg's neck prickled. The boy didn't understand. 'It helps me to not be late for anything. I can tell how long it is until the new year, for example.'

'Today is Last Moon an' tomorrow is the new year. Everyone knows that. Why do ya need sand to tell ya somethin' everyone already knows?'

Milo had a point, but it wasn't the right point. 'It can tell me other things, too. Like what year it is.'

'Ya don't know what year it is? I thought everyone knows that too. It's almost 947 after Division.'

'People only know because that's what everyone else tells each other. *This* invention of mine measures time. And time is very important,' said Cregg indignantly. He'd never tried to explain his calendar to anyone else before. His wife had shown an interest when she was alive, but dismissed it as nothing more than an activity to keep him busy and out from under her feet. As he now tried to explain it to Milo, the boy's questions unravelled every explanation he'd silently rehearsed to himself over the years. Time *was* important, even if it was harder to explain with actual words to a young boy. A slave child, no less.

'Why?'

Cregg rubbed his face with both hands. Why is *why* the most irritating of questions? As he drew in a deep breath to explain further, there was a knock at the door. Milo yelped and darted back behind the pillar, out of sight once again.

With his back still stiff from the fall, Cregg answered the door, and was surprised to find two men in black hooded robes standing at the threshold. *Tal Valar*. Without a word, they both pushed their way past Cregg, before turning to him and lowering their hoods. Cregg knew them both, by sight at least. He knew many of the Tal Valar, but none ever spoke their names. They were simply the Tal Valar and referred to each other only as "Brother."

'Gentlemen, I bid you welcome this fine Last Moon. How may I help you?' Only a fool would assume they were here for anything other than the boy.

'You're bleeding,' said the taller of the two, reaching out a finger towards Cregg's forehead.

'Am I? Oh, I'm afraid I had an unfortunate incident with

the steps.' He nodded at the broken glass scattered across the floor.

'One should not fear the unfortunate. Incident or otherwise.'

'Or otherwise,' echoed the second man. This brother looked almost a decade younger than the taller one. Both had shaved heads, including their eyebrows. Cregg knew of several pairings who shaved their hair in this way, though never learned why. Their complexion was pasty, and neither of them smiled.

Cregg rubbed at his ear with a finger. The Tal Valar always had an odd turn of phrase, but he learned to pay it no mind. 'How may I be of assistance?'

'We have reason to believe a young boy, wanted for thievery, came this way. He may be hiding somewhere nearby. Have you seen anyone of his like?'

'Of his like.' The younger of the two never spoke their own words, not in Cregg's experience, at least. It wasn't a habit unique to these two, either. All the Tal Valar were the same. It was as though they were linked somehow, in a broken kind of way.

'I've not seen anyone for two days. I haven't left the tower.' He hadn't intended on lying, but those were the words that left his mouth anyway.

Both the Tal Valar stared at him with matching suspicious expressions. Cregg held his nerve in silence and tried hard not to blink. *Can they tell I'm lying? That I'm harbouring a criminal child less than ten paces away?* He hoped not. As the taller brother opened his mouth to speak again, there was a crash of something metallic hitting the stone floor. This was followed by a blur of blond hair and rags darting out of the shadows. The boy barrelled into Cregg, almost knocking him off his feet, before making his escape through the door. The entire event was over in less than five seconds, and long before any of the three men had any clue what was happening.

'I had no idea he was there,' protested Cregg, trying his best to act surprised. In truth, he was, but only by the sheer nerve the lad had for making a run for it. *Probably for the best.* 'Is that who you are searching for? Had I have known...'

The brothers ignored him, gathered their wits, and made their own way out of the tower in pursuit of their prey. 'We will return for a statement,' the tall one said without looking back as they exited.

'For a statement.'

And that was that. The whole encounter was over. Thinking about it, it was the most exciting thing to happen to Cregg in a long time. He didn't like excitement.

3

Routine had been disrupted, and that didn't sit easily with Cregg. He adored routine. Every day started the same, played out the same, and ended the same. It helped him keep track of time and ensure the bell rang out across the city exactly when it needed to. Today, that routine was broken—as was, he felt, his body—and he resolved to catch up by mid-moon in the hope of a perfectly routine remainder of the day until moonset.

Leaving the comforts of his tower, as sparse and simple as they were, was not something he liked to do. Leaving the tower on Last Moon would be even worse. The sound of excited chatter permeated the air before he'd even opened the door. Miar Lenns was a busy city at the best of times. Today, well, today was the one day of the year when it seemed like the whole of Moranza crammed themselves into the winding streets of the city all at once. Lingering amongst the noise was the smell. It was a dense mix of dry, dusty air, body odour, sweat, and food—both fresh *and* stale—inter-twined with the latest developments in fire-retardant chemicals that were rinsed through anything combustible. Most of those smelled of rotting meat, and no amount of flower oil would disguise it.

Despite his preference for solitude, Cregg was well known and respected throughout the city, especially in the mile or so around the tower. Everyone knew him or knew *of* him. Often, he would even remember their names, too. It made going about his own business take twice as long, as they would all stop him for a chat, or pay their respects to his late wife, even all these years after her passing.

For as much as he liked the people he came across every day, he cared little about the city itself. A permanent breeze blew through the haphazardly constructed sandstone buildings, and it hadn't rained for one hundred and thirteen days now. He'd counted. That meant everything was so dusty, and the wind carried that dust in the air and stung his eyes, despite his best efforts to shield them as he walked. The palace would officially declare a drought soon, he was certain of that.

The market district was too busy for his liking. It was difficult to avoid physical contact with others as they brushed past, each trying their best to get through their own days unscathed. Some grumbled, whilst others acted as though they hadn't seen or felt their clipping of shoulders as they went by.

The noise was something else. Young children cried, and hawkers shouted their wares to anyone who would listen. Above the din, an air of excitement for the festivities due at the end of the day was felt by all. Cregg, of course, would watch the celebrations from the top of the tower. On his own. Something he had done every year since Petral died.

For him, it was a time for reflection, for fond memories of better times.

'Can I interest you in a new feather for your hat?' asked a small woman with a handful of brightly coloured feathers clutched tightly in her hand. She plucked one of them out, a bright yellow, and tickled Cregg's ear with it.

'You are most kind to offer, my dear,' he said, 'but as you can see, I have no hat.'

'In that case,' said the woman, unperturbed, 'perhaps I could sell you a hat? I have many inside my shop here. All kinds, and I'm certain we can find one that suits a gentleman of your stature.'

Cregg smiled and declined the woman's offer. Petral would have bought him one. She liked it when he wore a hat. They made his head itch, so the only time he wore one was on the most special of occasions. It had been so long since he'd had one of those.

On an average day, a visit to the market meant buying only food. In his old age, he enjoyed a simple life and required little in the way of possession or comfort. His clothes were old and threadbare, but they were comfortable, so he saw little point in buying new ones. Today, he needed new glass to construct a new timer. This need took him to the far end of the market, which meant a longer walk back to the tower afterwards. A walk he didn't have time for. He looked to the sky and regarded the moon. It wouldn't be long before it reached its apex, and he needed to be at the top of the tower, ready for that moment.

The market itself was an eclectic array of buildings and stalls. Some shops were little more than a stone box with a doorway, while others were metal-plated wooden shacks on wheels that were moved around the city wherever trade might be best. On the day of Last Moon, there were at least double the usual number of mobile traders. Some had come all the way from smaller provinces such as Min Brai or Miar Gelen hoping to make some extra money, much to the chagrin of the locals who were finding it increasingly difficult to make ends meet these days.

Everything one could want or need was on sale today. Cregg politely declined offers of clothing, hand-crafted metal effigies of the Architects, and food of questionable origin. He had no need for the latest fireproof washes, either. The old traditional solutions worked well enough for him, even if they did smell awful for the first day or two. No, he needed glass today, and glass only.

The shop he wanted was hidden behind a handful of wagons who had set up right outside, and the owner was far from happy.

'How is anyone meant to know I'm here with this rabble making a nuisance of themselves?' the owner grumbled, loud enough for the interlopers to hear him. He was perhaps even older than Cregg, who was already much older than he wanted to be. White wisps of hair stood in memory of a long-lost full head of locks, most of which had migrated to his eyebrows. Once, in years past, he'd have been strong and muscular. Old age ate away at him, a time-worn version of a younger man.

'Times are hard,' replied Cregg, stepping over a short stack of tin buckets blocking the way. 'Can you really blame them for trying to earn enough to get by?'

'Nah, but I would rather they did it elsewhere. You're the first patron I've had today, and it's almost mid-moon.'

Cregg glanced at the sky again. Time was indeed slipping

by. 'I require two glass bottles of this exact size.' He gestured with his hands to indicate his requirements.

'I have something that will suffice. Please do step inside.'

He followed the owner into his shop and was immediately hit by the heat. Miar Lenns wasn't a cold city, but the burning air inside was on another level, and sweat formed on his brow almost immediately. The shop itself was a picture of perfect organisation. Glass vessels of all shapes and sizes lined the walls on shallow shelves, all organised by size and by colour. There were other items too. Ornamental glass figurines depicting the Architects had their own small area, but it was the dragons that caught Cregg's eye. Dozens upon dozens of glass dragons of different sizes and colours took up a whole display near the furnace used to create them. Anything that created fire was illegal in the city without a special licence. The furnace itself was enclosed and posed no danger to its surroundings.

Cregg picked up a dragon figurine and turned it in the light. Reds and oranges twinkled within the glass as if it were alive. He liked it and reminded him of the one hidden in his tower. There was even a small amount of damage to one of the wings. 'How much for this?'

'Hum? Oh, three marks. Like dragons, do ya?'

'Only the non-dangerous ones.'

The shopkeeper nodded solemnly in agreement as he rummaged around of a shelf near the only window. 'I don't have any of the exact size you require. However, I do have these.' He held up two green flasks, wide at their base, and narrow as a wine bottle at the neck, one in each hand.

Cregg grunted. 'How long would it take to make what I need, precisely?'

'Precisely? Three days. Maybe two, if business remains as slack as this.'

That was too long to be without time. No, the green ones would have to do for now. 'Fine. Please make what I need and I'll take those. And the dragon.'

'Ten marks. Plus another fifteen for the new ones.'

'Twenty-five? Burn the stones!' Cregg shook his head as he fumbled for coin in his pocket.

'Times is hard. I need to eat.'

'We all need to eat. With these prices, I'll likely starve.' He handed over the money, took his items and left under a cloud of annoyance, unsure if he'd been robbed or not.

The outside breeze scattered that cloud away, leaving the oppressive heat of the glassmaker's shop behind. He frowned at the sky. Not long until mid-moon, maybe an hour at most. In all his years, Cregg had never missed a bell-ringing, and today of all days would not be the first. He tucked the dragon into a pocket, and with a glass in each hand, he made to weave his way through the bustling market back to the tower.

Less than a minute later, in a brief instant of watching the moon and not where he was going, he slammed nose-first into a wall. Except it wasn't a wall at all. In surprise, he dropped the vessels, the sound of shattered glass echoing around him.

'Blast and buggery!' he shouted, ready to admonish whoever had got in his way. He had to crane his neck to see their face.

Towering above him stood the largest woman he'd ever met. Seven feet tall at least, with broad shoulders and short, messy blonde hair. She looked at Cregg with a curious expression, as if she was as surprised to find someone in their path as he was. 'My apologies,' she said, her voice softer than her size would suggest. 'Are you injured?'

Cregg stared forlornly at the broken glass. 'No. You owe me for new vials, though.'

'Alas, I do not carry money. I have little need for small pieces of metal. Some of them do look rather pretty, would you not agree?'

Cregg frowned. 'How do you pay for things, then? Like food. And other people's breakages.'

'I do not.'

'You don't what?'

'Eat,' she replied, as if the question was stupid.

Cregg scoffed. 'Of course you eat. You must do.'

'Why must I?'

'Everyone does!' He tried to shake off the confusing conversation and focus on the dilemma at hand. 'Besides, what am I meant to do with this now? I needed that. It was very important. I must keep time accurately. I must.' He glanced at the moon again, worriedly.

'Yes, of course. Time is very important to you. Important to Amser, too.' The woman paused. 'I will offer you an exchange. I will put right your damage if you patronise the establishment across the way for me.' She nodded at a narrow-fronted store that looked more neglected than those either side of it. The windows were too filthy to see through, and from where he was standing, he couldn't tell what service the shop offered.

'You want me to go in there? Why?'

'Because I asked you to.'

Cregg scratched at his nose. In all his long life, this was probably the strangest exchange with another person he'd ever had. And now was not the time for it. The way he saw it, he had two options. Do as the woman asked, and hope she was true to her word and get him more glass. *How, though? She already said she doesn't have any money.* Or cut his losses and get back to the tower in time for the bell, and buy them himself afterwards. There was something compelling about this stranger. Something that was pushing him to acquiesce. A feeling pulling him from deep inside. It was hypnotic.

'I require a... thimble,' she said.

'I haven't agreed yet.'

'Of course you have.'

'Have I?' Cregg scratched his nose again. Before he knew what was happening, he found himself pushing open the creaky metal-plated door to the shop.

If the smell of the city outside offended his senses, then the stench inside the shop was guilty of killing them outright. Any hint of saliva in his mouth disappeared immediately, exchanged for stinging tears that made it difficult to see. There was definitely decaying meat in this shop—the odour was unmistakable.

As he wiped away the tears with the back of his sleeve, he was met with the figure of a young boy standing stock still, holding a metal tray that suggested silver, but was likely a cheaper metal. Tin, perhaps. Mouth open and wide-eyed, the boy stared at Cregg in a mixture of shock and guilt.

'You again,' said Cregg.

The tray Milo held fell from his grasp and clattered on the floor, scattering its contents everywhere. Wet, slimy meat of a dubious nature splattered in all directions, with some even reaching the ceiling. Milo yelped and darted away from Cregg, and disappeared behind a curtain hiding a back room.

The brief silence broke with the shouting of a gruff,

angry voice. Cregg couldn't make out what the man was saying, and instinctively edged closer to the curtain. It was none of his business, but curiosity got the better of him. The unseen man had a lot to say—or shout—and between the indistinct words, there was whimpering from the boy, protesting against the tirade of verbal abuse.

A snapping sound followed. To Cregg, it reminded him of the crack of a whip, or a snap of leather against something soft. Then, silence.

As Cregg approached the curtain as close as he dared, the silence gave way to grumbling, followed by footsteps. Cregg doubled back and reached for the nearest object on a shelf he could find, and pretended to be interested in that and not the goings-on behind the curtain.

'Can I 'elp yer?' The curtain swished to the side, revealing a stocky, hairy mess of a man with a sweaty brow and flattened nose. His left arm was missing, replaced with some kind of crude mechanical contraption—made of patinated metal and wire—strapped to his shoulder. It almost looked like a real arm, but lacked the range of movement one of flesh offered. The man walked with a heavy limp, and Cregg wondered if there was a similarly false leg hiding under the filthy pants he wore. All in all, this man looked as unappealing as the rest of the shop.

'I ahh,' stammered Cregg. 'How much is this?' He proffered the item in his grasp, and only then did he realise what it was.

'The stryde 'ead? Twelve marks.' The man's voice still carried an air of foul temper from his unseen tirade.

Cregg replaced the bird's head on the shelf, then wiped his hand on his trouser leg. 'I'll think about it. What I really require is a thimble. Do you carry those at all?' The hairs on the back of his neck tickled, and he fought to hide a shudder. *Get what you came for and get out of here. Blasted woman and her thimble.*

'Ain't sure I 'ave any. Try the box behind yer.' The man waved his mechanical arm at the area behind Cregg. Before Cregg could reply, the man hollered, 'boy!'

The sudden yelling startled him.

'Boy! Get yer sorry backside out here and clean up this shit!'

Cregg swallowed and made for the indicated box. As he rummaged through its contents, he caught sight of the curtain from the corner of his eye. Milo emerged from behind it, an old broom in his hand. The man clumped the boy on the back of the head as he passed.

There weren't any thimbles in the box, and Cregg had no willingness to continue searching. If the woman wanted one that badly, she would have to find one herself. New glass be damned, he'd buy his own. As he turned to leave, he saw Milo's face. The boy's left eye was puffing up, and a line of blood trickled from his nostril on the same side. Cregg gasped.

'Summing ter say?'

Cregg wanted to say a lot, but hesitated. He looked at the sorry state of Milo, then back at the man. He swallowed and shook his head. 'I, ahh, didn't find any thimbles. I'll try somewhere else. Thank you for your time.' Hurriedly, he made for the door and left.

Outside, in the thrum of the market quarter, there was no sign of the woman. She should have been easy to spot, given her stature, but there was no one around even remotely as tall as her. She was gone. Cregg scratched at his neck before remembering how grimy it was in the shop, again wiping his hands on his trousers in a futile attempt to remove the feeling of uncleanliness.

What was the point in all that? He grumbled to himself silently as he moved away from the shop, making a mental note never to go near the place again. *Did I imagine the woman?* No, the shattered glass still lay amongst the cobbles of the street, crunching under the boots of passers-by who didn't notice it. He looked around again for the woman without success.

Another glance at the sky told him there wasn't any more time to re-purchase what he required. The moon would soon reach its apex, so he'd have to venture out again later.

'Hello,' came a soft voice from behind him as he made his way through the market. The voice barely registered with him above the din, his thoughts of the boy weighing heavily on him.

Something tugged at the bottom of his shirt. 'Hello,' said the voice again.

He stopped and turned, and his gaze fell on a young girl of eight, maybe nine years old. She looked up at him with a grin, still tugging away at his clothing.

'Can I help you, young miss?'

The girl had messy tan hair that matched her complexion, but was otherwise clean and well-looked after. Although, she did appear to be on her own. 'This is for you,' she said, holding out a bundle of cloth.

'For me? What is it?' He took the bundle from the girl and peeled back the coarse cloth, revealing two glass vials identical to the ones he'd bought and dropped earlier. He looked at the girl, an eyebrow raised. 'I don't understand.'

'She said these are for you, and that you need to do the

right thing,' said the girl proudly, as if reciting a well-rehearsed poem. She giggled and then ran away.

Cregg looked around him for the mysterious woman. Again, he was frustrated. *Who was she? And what did she mean by "do the right thing?"* It wasn't even mid-moon, and the day was already giving him a headache. He'd had some odd experiences in his life, and none were anything he would care to admit to anyone else. Today? That was different. He didn't like it. Not one bit.

New glass in hand, clutched tightly in the cloth wrapping so as not to drop it a second time, he returned to the tower.

4

The old and worn out dragon stared back at Cregg from its crevice in the wall. It still hadn't eaten the last of the meat he'd given it earlier, and the creature looked tired. 'I've brought you something,' Cregg said. He removed the glass figurine from his pocket and placed it alongside his one-winged companion. The glass dragon looked almost lifelike itself, a smaller, more complete imitation of the real thing.

At first, the dragon seemed interested, circling around the inanimate visitor to its makeshift home. It sniffed at it, then, as if realising it wasn't real, it coughed out the tiniest amount of saliva—which produced nothing more than a faint wisp of smoke—before sweeping its long slender tail in displeasure at the false dragon. The figurine fell from the wall and shattered into dozens of fragments at Cregg's feet.

'That's gratitude for you,' he mumbled, shaking his head.

The dragon, stretched its remaining wing, looked at Cregg, then at the destruction, then back at Cregg before curling up back to sleep.

Despite the events in the market and not having a functioning timer, he was early. As a best guess, early by a whole quarter hour, which was far better than being late. It gave him a little time to think as he watched the bustling city below.

To the east, the sun remained hidden, as it always was. The sun was named Father, and he remained out of sight below the horizon. If one were to travel to Miar Miall—the farthest city on the edge of the world between the Eastern Plains to the north and Abbalon to the south—and looked out from the tallest building there, it is said you could see the very top edge of Father. His bright red colour gave the sky its orange hue and painted the moon herself pink. Of course, many have tried to venture farther east to glimpse more of the sun, but all succumbed to the intense heat. Indeed, the queen's late husband tried himself, and it killed him.

He looked west, towards the lost lands—once part of Moranza—now severed by the Division almost a thousand years ago. The queen had ordered a bridge built across the great chasm known as the Divide. On a clear day, he was convinced he could see snow in the far distance, and often imagined if life was so different there.

As he stared out across the vista, waiting for the moon, he couldn't shake the words the girl spoke when she handed him the new glass. *Do the right thing.* Those were the words of the strange woman. She sent him into the shop on a fool's errand, only to find the same young lad who had hidden himself away in the tower. *That couldn't have been a coincidence. Could it?*

If the Tal Valar were to be believed, the boy was a criminal, even if only a petty one. Yet, he was also the slave of the shop owner, and thus likely working on his instruction.

Orphaned children often ended up that way. He disagreed with the concept of slavery. It didn't sit right with him, nor Petral, but that was the way of the world. Especially in these modern times. These poorer times.

The dragon squawked and flapped its good wing, breaking him away from his thoughts. He looked at the moon. It was time, and it was as if the dragon understood the task at hand. He raised his hammer and struck the bell.

Do the right thing.

As the sound of metal on metal rang out over the city, he knew what he had to do. He had to go back. He had to save the boy from that man, he was sure of it.

Cregg walked with purpose—as best he could with old and aching bones—through the city, ignoring everyone on the way. He would not be stopped. He would not be distracted. Not this time. By the time he reached the shop, he still hadn't figured out exactly *what* he was going to do, or say.

Less than two hours ago, he'd vowed never to enter these premises again, such was how the experience went. Yet, here he was. Eyes closed, and a grimace on his face, he pushed open the door and stepped inside.

Somehow, the air smelled—and tasted—worse than last time, probably only because he already had a sick feeling in his stomach. There was no sign of the boy, nor the owner. Evidence of the dropped tray remained in some places, as though only hastily cleaned away.

This was a bad idea. Cregg half-turned to leave before he was noticed, ready to forget the whole idea. *The woman probably meant something else*, he reasoned, trying to talk himself out of it. Before his hand touched the door handle, the voice of the keeper rattled behind him.

'Back so soon? Always a pleasure ter see a returnin' customer.' The man's tone was coarse, laced with only a hint of sarcasm.

Cregg turned to him and forced a small smile. 'I, ahh, wanted to ask...' his voice was quiet, unsure. He still didn't know what to do.

The curtain to the back area rippled to the side and Milo stepped through from behind it. His left eye shone with a large angry bruise. In the time it had taken Cregg to ring the bell and return, the boy's injury had established itself firmly. The pain in Milo's expression was just as visible.

Cregg's back immediately stiffened at the sight of the lad. 'The boy,' he stated.

'What about 'im?' The man turned to Milo, who instinctively shrank back into the protection of the curtain.

'He is your slave, I presume?'

'Yeah, what's it ter you?'

'You shouldn't treat him like that. It's not right.'

'Is that so? What's it ter you how I treat me own property?'

'It's wrong. I should inform the Tal Valar about your mistreatment.'

The man roared with laughter. 'And tell 'em what? I done nothin' illegal. The boy on the other 'and, now the Tal Valar would be very keen ter 'ave 'im. Little thief that he is.'

'No doubt a thief only because he does your bidding.'

'And?'

'I...' Cregg hesitated, mouth open slightly. *Do the right thing.* 'I wish to buy him from you.'

The man pulled his head back as if it was the last thing

he expected to hear. 'Plenty of slaves for sale in the West District. Find yer own.'

Cregg stood firm, finding a backbone he never knew he had. 'No. I want this one.' He nodded at Milo.

'He ain't for sale. Why the interest in 'im?'

'I don't like the way you treat him. I mean, look at the state of him.'

Milo alternated looks between his master and Cregg, a mixture of fear and hopeful expectation.

'Like I say, he ain't fer sale, and I thank yer for mindin' yer own business. If you know what's good for yer, yer'll leave right now.'

Undeterred, Cregg reached into his pocket and produced a handful of coin. It was everything he had, which wasn't much. His hand trembled as he offered the money forward. 'I can pay for him, see?'

The man eyed the coin greedily for a moment before sniffing and waving the money away. 'Not enough.'

The notion of trading money for the life of another human being tore away at Cregg's conscience. It didn't sit right with him, and never had. Treating someone as little more—or sometimes even less than—a possession highlighted the very worst in society. Yet, here he stood, offering away all his money for the life of a boy he only barely knew the name of. Why? Pity? He'd witnessed slave mistreatment on many occasions, and was glad to have never become numb to it. *Do the right thing.* No, he was here because of her.

'What will it take? I'll not leave here without him.' It took every ounce of determination to sound strong enough to mean every word. Truthfully, if the man so chose, he'd likely kill him with his bare hands, mechanical or otherwise.

The man wrinkled his nose in thought. 'Dragon egg,' he said.

'Excuse me?'

'That's the price for the boy. One dragon egg. Bring me one by moonset bell and I will *consider* releasing the boy.'

In all his years, Cregg had never seen a dragon egg, and certainly didn't know where he would find one. Where did dragons nest, anyway? The only time anyone saw the dragons was when they swarmed the city. Or, in his case, when they turned up dead or injured. As he thought about it, he didn't even know what a dragon egg *looked* like. 'How do I...'

'Ain't my problem. If yer want the boy, that's the price. Take it or leave it.' The man wore a self-satisfied smirk. He knew what he was asking, and the futility of it. An impossible price, just to get rid of the old stranger in front of him trying to take away his slave.

Do the right thing. 'Yes, fine. By the bell. I will find you a dragon egg in exchange for the boy.' Cregg tried to sound confident. In this moment, he wasn't buying the boy... only time.

'Be off with yer, then. Go on, out with yer. No egg, no boy, an' don't be comin' back without one.'

Cregg looked at Milo. The lad looked so frail and scared, yet there was hope in his eyes as he silently watched his would-be rescuer. 'I will return. You can be sure of it.' The words caught on the back of his throat. He fumbled with the door handle and left the shop to the sound of mocking laughter from the man behind him.

～

The relative safety of the outside air did nothing to calm his nerves. It would probably be best to forget the whole thing and go back to the tower. Best for who, though? What was it about this boy? Why did he care so much about his fate? And suppose he somehow did find a dragon egg and buy the lad's freedom. What then? He was too old to be a guardian to another child. His own children had long since become adults themselves and left. His wife was no longer here, either. No, he was too old now.

Do the right thing. The words echoed around his head over and over. Was it the right thing? He no longer knew.

'You look like you lost a mark and not even found a penny,' came a woman's voice. Elderly and soft.

'Hmm?' Cregg looked for who spoke and saw the wrinkled eyes of a woman carrying a basket of wares looking up at him. She was one of the many traders who couldn't afford a standing market pitch, so carried everything around with them. The compromise was they could take their trade *to* their potential customers. Sometimes this was an advantage. There were strict limits, though. No trading was allowed outside the market perimeter, and this rule was enforced by the Tal Valar. As was everything in the city.

'Something is on your mind. I can tell. Perhaps I can interest you in some nice soothing salts? They'll help clear you of all that ails you.'

'No, thank you.' His reply was dismissive, his thoughts elsewhere.

'I have some nice moon cedar bark. Good for chewing.' The woman reached into her basket and produced a sorry-looking twig and waved it under his nose.

'Please,' he said, pushing her arm away and wincing at the bitter smell of the wood. 'I'm in no mood to purchase anything today. Unless... you have a dragon egg if that basket of yours?' He didn't expect her to have one of those, really.

'Ohh, a dragon egg, you say? Such a rare and expensive delight,' cooed the woman, her eyes brightening. 'Now, what would a man such as yourself do with a dragon egg?'

'You have one?' For a moment, his heart lifted.

'Ha! No. If I had me a dragon egg, I would not be dragging all this nonsense around with me every day, breaking my back—which is already broken. Broken, I say—trying to get by. No, I'd be right and retire to Min Brai and live out the rest of my days. Nice house, garden by the river. That's what I'd do if I had me a dragon egg.'

'Of course, how silly of me to even ask,' Cregg replied as he stepped away.

The woman pulled at his sleeve. 'Why would you be needing a dragon egg?'

'It doesn't matter,' he said, wrestling his arm from her grip. It *did* matter. It mattered to Milo. *For* Milo.

A pair of Tal Valar robes appeared from behind a nearby wagon laden with colourful fabrics. 'Is this woman bothering you?'

'Bothering you?'

'No, brother, not in the slightest,' said Cregg as the woman shrank away and scurried off to find her next customer.

The two Tal Valar brothers nodded and continued on their way without another word. They weren't the same pair who visited the tower earlier, searching for Milo. For all their strictness, it was merely the presence that instilled order in the city. A scuffle could break out and then evaporate instantly at the sight of them. You could go all day without seeing a single pair, yet you could count on them showing up at the slightest sign of trouble. It was uncanny, and they always made Cregg feel uncomfortable, as if instilling an unnatural dread within him.

Do the right thing. The stranger's words gnawed away at him once again. He was lost, unsure of what to do next. 'I tried,' he whispered to himself. 'What else can I do?' He resigned himself to returning to the tower, alone. He felt bad for the lad, he truly did.

'Psst!'

The sound briefly caught his attention above the hum of the market, but barely. Another noise amongst many.

'Psst! Mister tower man.'

Cregg stopped still. That *did* catch his attention, completely and with both hands. He jerked his head left and right, turning a full circle where he stood, searching for the voice calling him.

'Over 'ere.'

He followed the words beyond the milling crowd and between a stall selling vegetables and another offering an array of metal utensils. In the shadows between the two, a mere glimpse of blond hair, hiding. And then a hand, waving at Cregg.

It was Milo, he was sure of it. With a furrowed brow, he pushed his way through the crowd, ignored the owner of the vegetable stall owner as she waved an unusually large carrot at him, and caught up with the boy. Cregg considered if this was some sort of trap, with Milo's master lurking in the darkness, ready to strike him over the head and relieve him of his money. He brushed the thought aside, satisfied the boy was alone.

'Why'd ya do that?' asked Milo.

Cregg pointed at the angry bruise smothering Milo's eye. 'That's why. No one should be treated that way, slave or not.'

'And you didn't rat me out to the Tal Valar either. Why?'

Again with the why. 'Honestly, I don't know why. It felt like the right thing to do.'

'That was very... kind of you.'

His turn now. 'Why are we in a dark alley?'

'I came to help ya. Help ya help me. There's no way ya managin' on ya own.'

'Help me how?' The young lad was a curious one, in many ways. Cregg didn't mind admitting to himself he'd taken a liking to him, right from when he took interest in the calendar. Even if his endless inquisitions got on his nerves.

'I know where to find a dragon egg.'

5

When all was said and done, Cregg didn't have a lot of choice other than to follow Milo. It was a curious turn of events. To save the lad from that awful man, he had to find a dragon egg. Except, it turned out the only way he'd find one was with Milo's assistance. The boy was saving himself in a way.

'If you know where to find an egg, why can't you buy your own freedom?' Cregg asked as he tried to keep up with the boy as he weaved his way through the city.

'Anythin' I find is already his,' Milo said with a shrug, not turning back. 'I find 'im stuff all the time.'

'I see.' He didn't.

'Dragon eggs are worth a lot of marks. Hard to find, unless ya know where ya lookin'.'

'Have you not thought about taking one and running away? If they're so valuable, you could start a new life.'

Milo stopped and turned to Cregg. He looked confused. 'Where would I go? I don't have anyone besides Werral. He owns me, and if I ran away, it would be like stealin' from him.'

'You steal *for* him.'

'That's different. I have to do as I'm told. He tells me what to do, and I do it, else...'

Cregg knew what he meant.

'And if I ran away, I'd have all the Tal Valar lookin' for me *all* the time.'

'They're looking for you already.'

Milo resumed walking. 'They'll forget about this mornin' soon enough. I didn't even steal anythin'. Spotted before I had the chance. Nosey woman that she was, screamin' her 'ead off before I done nothin'.' He paused. 'Ain't important, anyway. Stealin' a master's slave. That's very important.'

'I'm sure you can't steal yourself.'

'Course ya can. There's rules and stuff. Laws.'

'Where are we going?' Cregg was already out of breath, and was farther away from the tower than he had been in years, if ever.

'Ya'll see.'

Cregg glanced at the sky to check the progress of the moon. The irony of that man's—Werral's—time limit was not lost on him. Return with an egg before the bell tolls. Except, he was the one who rings the bell, and he wondered if Werral knew that, somehow. Either way, he would return to the top of the tower this evening, with Milo freed, or as a failure.

Milo was leading him north. The only other people they came across on their journey were all heading into the city centre for the celebrations. The farther they walked, the quieter the streets became, and with no sign of Milo stopping, he grew concerned they wouldn't return in time.

Eventually, and after traversing a narrow path that looked untrodden for years, Milo stopped, turned to Cregg, and smiled. 'Here.'

'Where are we?'

The lad stopped at a broken wall covered in foliage that was once alive, now merely a memory of the growth it once had. The wall itself was of the same sandstone as the majority of Miar Lenns, though disrepair and age had claimed it. Wherever this was, it had long since been abandoned. There were signs of scorching in places—a telling sign of dragon activity. Some of the marks looked rather recent. Cregg shuddered.

Milo moved off again, hand to the wall, running his fingers up and down as they followed the cracks in the surface. Cregg must have blinked at the wrong moment as the boy disappeared, and he didn't see where. Then, Milo's head appeared from a hole in the wall. 'Are ya comin' or not?'

The hole was low to the ground, and not very large. As he did his best to squeeze through, with small pieces of sandstone and a lot of dust pulling away from the structure, Cregg wished he was thinner. Indeed, once he was as thin as the boy he was following. Advancing years and too much food had changed all that. And then he was stuck. At the waist.

Milo doubled back on himself from the other side, laughing at Cregg's misfortune, and reached out a hand. Once again, the lad was the one doing the help. Maybe it would have been better to have minded his own business and not bartered for Milo's freedom. *Too late now, I'm here. Wherever here is.*

With more effort than he would have liked to save embarrassment, he conquered the hole in the wall. Cregg was once again upright, only now with a little less dignity. He dusted himself down and took in his new surroundings. He was surprised to find they were not alone.

Before them stood a decrepit and abandoned building. Once, a long time ago, this would have been a Tal Valar prayer lodge. He recognised the design of the only section of roof that remained intact. *Definitely Tal Valar.* A significant portion of the structure was wooden, with a sandstone shell. Construction from wood had been banned for centuries, such was the influence of the constant dragon swarm attacks. No, this place was far older than anything else in the city by some margin.

Amongst the debris, dried foliage and other broken things were a number of people huddled in the shadows. They were all as dishevelled as the hidden world around them, and none paid any attention to Milo or Cregg.

'What is this place?' Cregg asked.

'The place no one remembers,' replied Milo nonchalantly. 'Strange things happen here. Magic things. Notice how the wind doesn't come here?'

He hadn't noticed. Not until he mentioned it. There was *always* wind. An ever-present gentle breeze that pulsed through the air every day, always in the same direction. Here, this side of the wall? There was none. The air was perfectly still, as if inside a building without doors or windows. Silent. Cregg didn't like it, as if an essential part of one's soul had been hidden away. He shivered.

There weren't any dragons. None that he could see, at least. Given their size, it was difficult to spot them at the best of times.

'They're hard to see, the dragons,' said Milo, as if reading his mind. 'Always starts with just one, but there's always more. Two, then three, and then a whole swarm of them everywhere, destroyin' everythin'.' He waved his arms around animatedly for effect, a broad grin on his face.

'I'm well aware of how much trouble they are.' Cregg had lost count of the number of attacks he'd witnessed in his life. *There's always more.* Those words snagged in his mind. The lad was right.

Little remained written of history, though some spoken stories say the dragons arrived with the Divide. Some say they come *from* the Divide somehow. No one was absolutely sure. They may have been around since the Architects created the world, for all Cregg knew. What was well-known was the *fear* when talking about them.

'Who are those people?' Cregg asked as he followed Milo over broken rubble towards the building. The structure had no roof left, and most of the south-facing wall had collapsed, exposing rotted wooden beams where a floor between upper and lower levels had once been. Dark green and purple plant-life wrapped around the remains, possibly being all that held it together, now.

'The Forgotten,' said Milo softly, as one might talk about the recently deceased. 'They have nothin'. No one. Not their fault, either.'

'The dragons don't scare them?'

'Nah. Dragons ain't scary, really. Misunderstood, I think.'

As they clambered through the ruins, Cregg's eyes locked with one of the "forgotten", a woman of middling age. Her face was gaunt, her lips tight against her teeth. There was no emotion in her expression, as if her body was completely vacant. As if she had forgotten how to die. Cregg smiled weakly at her, but received no reaction other than her following his movements.

'They don't talk. Never heard any of them say nothin'.'

'Can't anyone help them?'

'Nobody comes. Everythin' here, everyone, is forgotten.'

'You come here. Why?'

Milo only shrugged, not saying a word.

A second figure, wrapped in an old and tattered blanket speckled with mould, caught his eye. This one was different. Not human. He recognised the grey, mottled skin and over-sized ears of a gabbalin male. They looked malnourished at the best of times—barely more than skin and bone—but this one looked as empty as the others. The gabbalin didn't look at Cregg, only staring into the orange sky, neck craned upwards, nestled against the rough wall behind where he sat.

Only once in his life had he spoken to a gabbalin. He recalled the strange vibration in her voice. She was nice enough, though very secretive. They all were, never speaking about their home, Abbalon, despite all being exiles. The encounter had sparked a curiosity in him for a while, eager to learn more about them. He discovered very little, in the end. Nothing was written about them, and they refused to talk about themselves. They simply existed in small groups, often ignored or despised by the rest of humanity. Exiled from their own home, unwelcome in their new. It irked him that he never found out more.

'I don't like it here,' he muttered.

'Why not? I come here all the time. It works better here.'

'What works better?'

'Ya'll see.' Milo hopped from loose rock to loose rock, almost in a dance without a song.

The more Cregg paid attention, the more people he found. Dozens of them. Most were sitting, or curled up, on the ground. One or two meandered around the ruins, aimless. It looked like a real-life sketching of the end of times, complete with a stale smell in the unmoving air. A sense of nothingness pulled at his very being, threatening to make him like them if he stayed too long. Milo looked completely unfazed by it all. Happier even.

It was only once the two of them had entered the bowels of the building did Cregg see the first dragon. They were walking through what could have once been a kitchen, and there it was, perched high on the jagged edge of a stone in the wall. Its red scales looked more the colour of dried blood against the shadows, with winged forearms tucked tight against its body. Two small black eyes observed them with caution. Dragons didn't have a brow as such, but if they did, then this one would be frowning, wary of the intrusion.

'We need to get up there,' stated Milo, pointing to the next level.

There was no obvious way to get to where the boy indicated. There were no steps. Presumably, there had been, once. Cregg considered he was probably standing amongst the remains of them. 'How?'

'We climb.'

'Climb? If you haven't noticed, I am of no fit age to climb anywhere,' he performed a gesture with both hands to show his stature and how unsuitable it was for anything other than sitting down.

Milo smiled and rolled his eyes. 'There is always a way. Watch. I'll show ya a secret.'

An intense look of concentration came over Milo and he reached out an arm, pointing to a charred, but intact, wooden beam. Cregg was about to ask what the lad meant, but his mouth fell open when the beam moved. Ever so slowly, it scraped and bounced over the rubble until it leant diagonally against the wall.

'Burn the stones! What in the name of the Architects was that?'

'I can move stuff by thinkin' about it. Mostly small things, except here. Somethin' about this place makes stuff lighter.' Still grinning, Milo hopped onto the beam, bounced on his heels to check it was sturdy enough, then walked to the top, jumped and pulled himself up onto the upper level of the ruined building. His movements sent dust billowing into the air. Without the breeze, the dust hung like a cloud. All the while, the dragon watched, making only tiny clicking noises with its sharp talons against the stone.

'I've lived long enough to have seen most things. This, this... I have no words.'

'Come on,' said Milo, waving Cregg to him. 'Your turn.'

'I think I'll stay down here, if it's all the same to you.'

'You ain't findin' no dragon eggs down there.'

The forgotten body of a man staggered past between Cregg and the beam like a twig moving down a stream, paying no attention to what was going on around him. Cregg considered whether the man was actually dead. *Poor chap, he may as well be.* He shuddered and looked at the beam.

'All this is for you anyway,' said Cregg, shaking his head.

He took hold of the beam with both hands, holding as tightly as he could, and gingerly put one foot on. It took all the effort he could muster not to topple head-first over the other side. He puffed his cheeks and held still, willing his body to find balance with the wood. Cursing under his breath, he moved, inch by inch, towards Milo, who was lying with his chest to the floor, watching the comedy act beneath him.

'I'm too old for this,' he protested.

Milo reached out a scrawny hand and helped Cregg steady himself as he clambered to the upper level. The room that had once been there, now an open platform to the sky, looked... unsafe. Gaps in the flooring threatened to return them both to the ground far faster than they'd climbed. Perhaps this once had been a bedchamber, though there was no furniture left to confirm that.

The dragon—if it was the same one—chirped quietly from its stone perch on the far side. Watching with interest. Cregg stepped forward, placing his feet tentatively, one in front of the other, testing the strength of the floor before putting his full weight down. He winced at the sound of the floor creaking under his feet. The dragon squawked and ruffled its wings, as if a warning. He hesitated, taking heed.

The boy had no such trepidation. He hopped and skipped over any obstacle in his way, almost dancing across to the other side. There was nothing to him, the danger of the floor giving way beneath him minimal. Cregg regretted the years of extra food and ales. What he wouldn't give right now for one of his wife's meat pies. She adored cooking for him. He swallowed a mouthful of saliva. No pie had ever tasted quite the same since she died.

'We don't have long left, so ya better hurry,' shouted Milo from the other end of the room.

He was right. The moon was a barely more than a quarter full now, no need to crane his neck to see it in the sky. Cregg shook his head, held his arms out to the side for extra balance, and tip-toed his way over. The other side didn't feel any less safe once he got there, and he put the thought of having to go back across once they found an egg to the back of his mind.

'So then, you're certain there's a dragon egg here?'

Milo nodded furiously, smiling. 'Oh yes. There's always an egg. Ya'll see.'

The myriad of overgrowth covering what remained on the building hid a door, which Cregg only noticed when Milo pulled on it. It was old, wooden and heavy, judging by the effort it took Milo to open it even part way. It was rare to see a door that hadn't been plated to protect everything from fire. *Too late for that now.* Cregg decided this place wouldn't look so different if it *did* burn down.

Milo tugged on the door repeatedly, each time edging it open another inch or two. Behind them both, the dragon screamed furiously, agitated at their actions. Cregg followed the screeching, the tiny winged creature suspended in the air in the middle of the room, its wings beating, keeping it in one place. It kept on screaming, a warning, as if telling them both to go no farther. Milo ignored it, still attempting to wrench the door open. All Cregg could do was watch the dragon, unable to take his eyes off it, lest it swoop in and attack when his back was turned.

'This isn't a good idea,' protested Cregg, taking half a step backwards, minding where he put his feet still.

'It's almost open. Pay no mind to the dragon.'

'Dragons.' Cregg pointed to his left. There was now a second one, then a third. The adage was proving true. Where you see one dragon, there are always—always—more, unseen. Waiting. The minute beast was summoning others. Cregg gulped, sweat beading at his temples.

With one last heave, Milo almost fell backwards as the door finally relented and swung open. 'Inside, quickly, and close it behind you.' His instruction was insistent, but without panic.

Cregg did as the boy said and dashed through the open door and pulled it closed behind him without looking back to see if any more dragons had joined its friend. The wooden bulk of the door scraped and whined as it returned to its frame, and then it went dark. Wherever they were now, there were no windows. The ceiling was intact—not even a crack —as if this place were perfectly preserved in contrast to everything else.

6

'Milo?' Cregg ventured, trying to make out anything, anything at all. The darkness was absolute.

The boy didn't reply, only his footsteps echoed gently against their stone surroundings. Then, silence, followed by the appearance of a small blue-white light. A single speck of pure brightness floating in the air. It cast the cavern in a soft milky light with Milo at its centre, his shadow dancing on the ground behind him.

'Is that you? Are you making that light?' whispered Cregg.

'Of course it is. No one else down here except us. And the dragons, but they don't make light this way.'

'Well, burn the stones.' Cregg had heard the stories of certain folk being able to use magic. Never in all his years had he met one himself. As far as he understood, using magic hurt enough to deter its use. Children especially, as that is when it manifests itself. Every once in a while, though, the stories say, someone learns to accept that pain. Even so, the magic was so weak it was little more than a novelty act. So the stories say. 'Wait... what do you mean, down?'

'This is underneath. Outside is above, inside is below.'

'I don't understand.' Cregg took a step forward and banged his head on the low ceiling. 'Ow!'

'Something happened here. Long time ago. Something magic. Made everything broken. Made everything different. The dragons like it here.'

As they moved deeper into the cavern, it became apparent it wasn't a cavern at all. Once, long ago, this would have been a cellar. *Or a dungeon.* The walls were too neat and straight to be a cave. Someone had carved this space out of the ground and then built the structure over it. The place had an eerie feeling to it, as if it held stories that should never be told. Forgotten. Much like the poor people who lived above—or were they below? Their souls seemingly sucked out of their very existence.

'I don't see any dragons,' said Cregg. 'Are you sure we're in the right place?'

'Yes, of course. This is where the dragons live. This is where they all come from, and go to.'

'I thought they lived in the deserts of the Eastern Plains.'

'Some do, maybe.'

Cregg wondered how they got in and out. As best as he could tell, there was only the one door, and that was behind them. 'Where are they, then?'

'Can't you see them? They're everywhere.' Milo pointed to a crevice above him.

Cregg squinted, trying to focus on the detail of the walls against the glow of Milo's conjured light. Nothing. As far as he could tell, there was nothing there but rock.

And then the colour of the light changed. What was once

a soft blue-white light slowly morphed into a pale purple as Milo moved through. It pulsed gently. Brighter, then dimmer, carefully moving between the two. The light Milo had made blinked out, no longer required.

The purple light shimmered against the walls like moonlight on water. It was both beautiful and unsettling at the same time.

'What *is* that?' asked Cregg. A sliver of purple light, more intense than that cast around them caught his eye. He moved to it, crouched down, and reached out. It appeared to be a small crack in the rock surface, no longer than a finger and no wider than a hair. The light was intense, but it wasn't *bright*. Not like looking into fire. It was just... purple. A rich, vibrant purple. As he tried to touch it, his hand passed right through it as though it wasn't there.

'Dunno. It's what makes everythin' forgotten. What makes this place feel different. Weird, isn't it?'

'You're telling me!' Cregg waved his hand back and forth through the strand of light. It felt like nothing and everything, all at once.

Above them, a ripple of noise moved from left to right. Flapping. Cregg snapped his head away from the strand and tried to follow the sound. He caught sight of something small a fraction of an instant before it disappeared, taking the sound with it. Almost certainly it was a dragon.

'I don't like it here. Where is the egg?'

Milo pointed. 'In the nest. Up there.'

Cregg followed Milo's finger to a small ledge directly above the strand of purple light, as if it had been some sort of marker. 'How are you supposed to get up there?' He guessed the ledge, which looked unassuming and all but invisible against its surroundings, stood barely ten feet above them. There wasn't an obvious way up. The nearest wall was too smooth to climb—not that he had the physicality to do that anymore, if he ever did. No, Milo would need to get up there somehow.

'It's easy, but ya have to be careful. Dragons are very protective of their nest.'

Nest—singular. More movement from above, and potentially more than one dragon. Cregg's heart pounded against his ribs. Milo looked at him expectantly. 'Me? You expect *me* to climb up there? No way. Uh uh.' He waved both hands in protest.

'It's easy. Ya can do it.'

'I absolutely cannot. Why can't you go? I thought you do this all the time? That's what you said.'

Milo shook his head. 'I never said that. I told you I knew where. I never actually stole one. They won't let me near the nest. Somethin' about my magic protects the egg. Ya don't have magic, so I think ya might do it.'

Cregg looked at the ledge again. 'There's no way up, so...'

'Jump. This place lets me move heavy things. If ya jump, I can help.'

'Who are you calling heavy?'

Milo giggled. 'Jump. I'll help. I promise.'

Why didn't I stay at the tower? Do the right thing, she said. Yeah, yeah, whatever. I'll show her the right thing. This is ridiculous! Cregg grumbled and muttered to himself as he tried to pull his thoughts into some semblance of sanity. 'Jump?' He shook his head, resigned. Milo nodded vigorously.

Cregg hopped once and nothing happened.

'Ya need to do it properly.'

Through a low growl, he bent his knees, unsure if they'd ever let him stand straight again, and pushed. Gravity didn't pull on him this time. He kept going up, as if falling in the wrong direction. Somehow, he found himself clinging to the edge of the ledge, astounded. For one brief second, he flew, and now he felt sick to the stomach.

Before today, he'd never considered what a dragon's nest would look like. The only living dragon he'd seen up close for any longer than a fleeting moment as it flew through the sky —usually among a swarm of thousands—slept at the top of his tower. It seemed perfectly happy in a small crevice between two stones. No bedding material like you would find with birds. Simply a bed of bare rock.

'You better have a safe way of getting me back down from here,' Cregg called.

On the ledge where he now found himself, and exactly above the thin thread of purple light, sat a circle of small gravel chips piled three fingers high and as wide as an average dinner plate. The purple light from beneath him shimmered against the wall and seemed to make the chips of rock glow—as if feeding off the light. In the centre of the circle was another stone. Only the one, and perfectly round and almost pure white except for the purple light cast over it.

'Can ya see the egg?' called Milo, out of sight below.

'I think so. There's a stone in the middle of a circle.'

'Yes, that's it. Ya will need to be quick. Don't let the dragons see ya take it. Otherwise...'

Cregg could imagine what "otherwise" meant. He didn't need to finish the sentence. There were dragons in the cellar with them. There was no doubt in his mind. How many? There was no way to tell. At least two, but there could be hundreds or more. Caution was needed here.

From his position, he studied the nest and the surrounding area. No signs of movement so far. Above the ledge, maybe another three or four feet, came the ceiling—not enough room to stand upright. It was too dark to see much detail of the stonework, though he tried to squint his way to seeing into the cracks nonetheless. That's where they would hide. That's where *he* would hide if he were so small. Nothing, though. No movement, no sounds. Milo shuffled impatiently below, but that was it.

He edged his way closer to the nest, as if sneaking up behind someone to surprise them, all the while keeping an eye out for any change around him. *Why am I up here instead of him?* He tried not to think how he would get back down. Carefully, he shimmied forward, mindful of the time he was taking, and how little of it he had.

Barely had he got within reach of the nest came the sound of faint clicking. No, not clicking—tapping, ahead to his right, and above. He looked to where the noise came from, but there was still nothing there, not that he could see. He could *hear* it, though. Click, click, *click*. It was as if it were a warning. Warning him not to go any farther. *Stay away from the nest.*

'There's something up here with me,' he whispered.

'Pardon? I can't hear ya,' shouted Milo.

Cregg cringed as the boy's voice reverberated against the walls. And there it was, perched on the far side of the nest. A single dragon, its winged forearms outstretched, with black, beady eyes staring at him. The creature held that post, its stare locked with Cregg's own, warning him not to come any closer. He imagined how fearsome these creatures would be if they were bigger. One tiny dragon wasn't much of a threat on its own, was it? Now, if it were the size of a tamewolf, *that* would be scary. *What if it were the size of a house, or even bigger?* He shuddered at the thought. No, this one tiny animal. He could handle that, if he was quick.

He tried shooing it away. Smaller creatures should fear things bigger than they were, right? The dragon didn't flinch. It remained—unmoved—wings still outstretched like it had become stone.

What to do? What to do? 'There's a dragon staring at me,' he hissed, hoping Milo could hear him.

'Only one? There's never only one. Ya need to hurry. Get the egg and get down.'

Easier said than done, lad. 'I should just grab the egg?'

'Yes!'

Cregg locked his eyes with those of the dragon, taking measure of where the egg was without looking at it. 'Easy now,' he whispered. 'I don't want to hurt you. That's it, stay where you are.' He tried to sound as soothing as possible. He'd heard stories of people who could talk to deadly snakes, hypnotising them to their will. Snakes weren't *that* different to dragons, were they? The dragon was having none of it.

The tiny creature screeched and flapped angry wings at Cregg, and then spat. A glob of clear liquid hurled from its mouth, landing in front of him, mere inches away. The liquid ignited on contact with the stone of the ledge, a small ball of orange fire created shadows around the nest. He pulled his arm back. *That was close!* The dragon was protecting its nest, of course it was. It could easily have spat at him directly, but it didn't. Another warning, more than simply trying to make itself appear bigger with its wings outstretched. He knew if the dragon spat at him again, he'd be in trouble.

The clothes he wore were washed in a fire-retardant dip —as was legally required, despite the smell. He couldn't afford the expensive stuff, and in all honesty, had no idea if the liquid actually worked, or simply smelled bad. No one would be keen to let a dragon set fire to them to test exactly how fireproof their clothes were, and only a fool would set fire to their own pants just to see if they were still wearable after.

This was it. Now or never. Cregg sucked in a lungful of stale air, steadied his nerves, and threw himself forward. With his right hand, he swiped at the dragon, striking it cleanly in the side of its body, sending it screeching into the air. He snatched the egg with his left hand a fraction of a second later. He was too quick, even for himself, and lost his balance, falling chest first into the nest.

'Have you got it?' called Milo.

'Yes,' groaned Cregg, his cheek pressed against the stone ledge, his whole body weight behind him.

'Then what are ya waitin' for? Get down from there. Let's go!'

Egg clutched in his hand, he grunted as he pushed himself away from the nest. The air around him echoed with the sound of the crying dragon. Except, it wasn't echoing. There was more than one dragon crying now. How many? *Too many!* He looked up to find not only the one he'd batted away, but a dozen more, all buzzing around him. Shielding his face with his arm as the dragons spat at him, he clambered his way down from the ledge, Milo's magic the only thing stopping him from falling altogether. Even with help, he still landed in a heap in front of Milo.

'No good lyin' around all day,' the boy joked as he grabbed Cregg by the armpit, helping him to his feet.

A shooting pain seared through his ankle. *I must have twisted it when I landed.* He limped after Milo back the way they came, wincing with each step as they went. Behind them, the dragons attacked. Together, they spat their little mouthfuls of liquid fire. For the most part, the protective wash stopped his clothes from catching alight. That protection didn't extend to his skin, though. A blob of dragon spit stuck to the back of his hand. Immediately it felt hot, and then came the flames. Cregg cried out as the burning liquid seared his skin. As he staggered through the cellar, he jammed his burning hand into his armpit and smothered the flame, dragon egg still in his grasp.

'We're going to die in here!' shouted Cregg.

'I think I can help,' replied Milo. He was ahead of Cregg, but stopped and turned back. 'Keep goin', get to the door.'

'What are you going to do?'

'Trust me, just get yaself out. I'll be right behind ya.'

Hand still tucked under his arm, Cregg hobbled past Milo, trying to find his way to the door. His whole body ached and burned and complained in agony. *Why did I agree to this? How had it come to this? That bloody woman. Do the right thing, she said. Well, the right thing is going to get me killed! Burn the bloody stones and that woman with them!*

The dragons continued their assault as he tried to run as best as he could. Though it hurt, he knew he hadn't broken his ankle. Honestly, the tumble down the steps of the tower this morning hurt more, but his age betrayed him.

He found the door and tried to open it, but it barely moved. Old and stiff, just like him, and he saw the irony in it. Behind, Milo shouted. Not at him as such. It was more of a growl, a mix of high pitch, and low rumble, his young years still discovering his adult voice. Cregg turned to find the lad crouched on the ground, pulling at it as if to uproot a weed. The dragons surrounded him—dozens of them—swooping and attacking. Milo had his head bowed, though he wasn't cowering from them.

A small light grew from the space Milo occupied, similar to the one he used to light the way when they first entered. Cregg moved away from the door, only for the boy to insist he exit the cavern. Milo had his back to him, so how could he see? The light grew until Cregg was forced to shield his eyes. Still the dragons kept coming, pelting Milo with fire. Yet, he did not burn. The small balls of fire didn't even touch him, as if there was an invisible shield around him. Then, Milo sprung up and out, the light bursting until everything turned white. And the screaming of the dragons stopped. *Silence.*

'That won't stop 'em for long,' said Milo, shaking his head furiously as if clearing away a morning fog.

'What was that?' asked Cregg, awestruck, fumbling for the door without looking at it, his gaze firmly on Milo.

'I told ya. Magic. It's stronger here. Much stronger. Somethin' to do with the dragons, I think. I used it to stop them. Stopped them dead. Not dead, dead, though. They'll keep comin'.'

'I don't doubt it,' said Cregg as he leaned into the door with his shoulder. Between the pair of them, the door eventually gave way. The fresh air of the outside world was a welcome respite, but only for a second.

It was as though the dragons had some kind of collective telepathy, as several were waiting for them as they exited. They began attacking the instant they were spotted. Screeching from within the cavern told them they couldn't go back, either. Whatever Milo had done to stop them had already worn off.

'We need to run. Once we are outside the wall, they'll

leave us alone,' said Milo, grabbing Cregg by his good hand and pulling him along.

'Are you sure? Are you certain they won't follow us?'

Milo hesitated before nodding with a smile. 'Almost sure. No choice either way. If we stay, they will burn us alive.'

Cregg had no argument with that. He pulled his coat over his head, shocked at how damaged it was. The dragon fire had burned through whatever protection the wash had offered, and the fabric had been singed in several places.

Together they ran, scrambling back to solid ground, over rubble and through debris. The inhabitants of this place, still in whatever stupor held them, ignored the chaos unfolding around them, as if they were in another world entirely. Cregg snagged his bad ankle on a loose stone and cursed his way through the pain. Fire rained down on them, and that was when he noticed—the remains of the building had caught alight. The wooden parts, as old and rotten as they were, had succumbed to the onslaught of the dragons.

And then Cregg saw something that made his blood run cold. One of the forgotten—a man of advancing years much like himself, except a lot less well-fed—caught fire. The flames enveloped his whole body so quickly there was nothing either he or Milo could do. The man didn't scream, didn't react in any way. He kept on ambling through the destruction around him until the flames consumed him, sending him to his death.

Cregg simply stood and watched, mouth open, aghast. It took Milo to pull him free of his dazed state and drag him to the hole in the wall. The lad practically shoved him through the not-quite-large-enough gap through to the other side.

On the ground once again, this time outside the perimeter of danger, Cregg forced himself to roll onto his back. He couldn't see the moon, which meant it was closer to the horizon. Time was running out. Milo stood over him, grinning. The lad did that more often now, he noticed.

'Ya fall over a lot,' Milo said, offering his hand.

'One day you'll be as old as I am. It's not easy to stay upright when your body betrays you.'

Milo shrugged. 'If ya say so.'

As Cregg got to his feet, he realised his hand hurt. He didn't recall injuring it, but as he looked at the back of his hand, he saw how red and angry it looked—as though it had been burned. He prodded at it, the skin puffy and welting. *What happened? How did I do that?*

Something scratched away at the back of his mind as he looked at the gap in the wall. They'd come out through that hole, *hadn't they?* He couldn't remember. The more he tried to concentrate, the harder it became to focus. He clearly remembered Milo telling him they had to go through the hole to find the dragon egg. There was a dragon egg in his pocket, so they *must* have gone in. Yet, there was nothing. It was as if the hole in the wall represented a hole in his memory.

'Were we...?'

'A strange place is that buildin'. Messes with ya brain. That's why no one goes in there. That's why no one sees this place. Except me. And I don't know why me, either. I'm the only one. To everyone else, it's forgotten.'

Forgotten. Now, there's a word that he thought should have some meaning to him. *Forgotten what?* He couldn't remember. Nor could he remember if he knew something he'd now forgotten. Were there really dragons in that place? He didn't see any, now that he thought about it. How lucky to get hold of a dragon egg and not have any bother from the creature that laid it. His hand *did* burn, though, and he'd done something to his ankle, too. *How did that happen?*

'Come on, we need to get back. I belong to ya now. Need to make it official.' Milo waved his arm, showing off the copper slave bracelet on his wrist. The metal had discoloured his skin around it green. His eagerness was on full display, all smiles and ill-fitting clothes.

Cregg retrieved the egg from his pocket, only then noticing the scorch marks on his coat. *Ruined.* Something happened back there, inside. He was sure of it.

Forgotten.

7

The nagging feeling in his mind kept on at him as they hurried their way back from the outskirts of the city to the market square. Milo spent most of the journey whistling and chatting to himself, declaring all the things he would like to do when he was no longer a slave to that awful man. For Cregg, the burning of his left hand kept his thoughts on what had happened, trying to force those memories to the surface.

'Ya shouldn't worry about it,' said Milo. 'There's no use tryin' to remember somethin' that that place won't let ya remember.'

'Do *you* remember what happened in there?'

'Nope. Don't care either. I know about that place. I know there's dragons in there. But I only know what's there when I'm there. Inside I remember. Outside, I forget.'

'Doesn't that bother you?'

'Why?'

There's that question again. 'It should bother you. It bothers me!'

The moon was less than half a quarter full as it hung low above the cityscape ahead of them. There was barely more than an hour left before Cregg would need to be back at the top of the tower, to ring the bell. To mark the end of the day —a day that he should forget, yet also struggled to recall in equal measure. He still hadn't worked out what to do with the boy once he'd exchanged the egg for his freedom. That, he decided, could wait until tomorrow. *One thing at a time.*

As the tower came into view, they were met by two robed figures walking in the opposite direction towards them. Cregg spotted them first, recognising them as the two who had come calling at the tower that morning... looking for Milo.

Neither had noticed them yet, but there was nowhere to go. No side alley to duck behind. He hadn't felt this guilty since he was a child, caught red-handed by a market trader stealing a piece of candied fruit. He'd done nothing like that since.

'Act like you haven't done anything wrong, and they'll ignore us,' whispered Cregg.

'Huh? Oh.'

The two robed figures nodded a shallow bow as their paths crossed. Cregg exhaled through his nose, eyes closed, and kept walking. He silently thanked the Architects the two Tal Valar didn't recognise them.

'Wait!'

His heart sank and his mouth went dry at the command. 'Run,' he hissed to Milo. 'Meet me at the tower.'

'Why?'

'Never mind why. Do as I say. I'll deal with them. Go!'

Eventually, after taking the hint, Milo broke into a run and disappeared into the city.

'Hey, you little bastard, get back here!' called Cregg before throwing his hands into the air. He turned to the two Tal Valar, who themselves had doubled back. Cregg prayed to whichever of the Architects was responsible for deceit that his ruse was convincing enough.

'It intrigues us that we should meet again, and that our fugitive should be in your company,' said the taller of the two robed men, his face a mere shadow beneath his hood.

'In your company.'

'Yes, I, ah, happened to come across the boy on my travels whilst visiting a friend. You have both known me a long time, and know my respect for the laws, and the Tal Valar, of course. I apprehended the thief myself and was bringing him to justice, and hand him to your care. Unfortunately, my age is getting the better of me and I didn't recognise you as we passed. As soon as you called, he bolted, and only then did I realise who you were. I must apologise.' Cregg lowered his head, hands clutched together despite the pain. He tried to keep the injury hidden so as not to draw more questions.

The two men lowered their hoods at the same time, perfectly synchronised and looked at each other, then looked at Cregg. The taller one cocked an eyebrow and eyed him curiously.

'That is unfortunate.'

'Unfortunate.'

Cregg nodded. 'Yes, most unfortunate indeed. Well, I must be going. It is nearly moonset and I must ring the bell on time. I am sure you understand.'

'Please do not presume to know what we understand and what we do not,' said the tall one, making a sweeping gesture with his hand, exposing a missing finger. 'Our lives are devoted to the true understanding of our nature and purpose in this world. The Architects themselves teach us we will never truly understand their plan for humanity.'

'For humanity.'

Cregg scratched his head nervously. He didn't have time for their predilection for twisting anything into a sermon and how they saw the world. 'Forgive me, my good friends...' he winced as soon as the words left his mouth.

'Forgiveness is to be sought only from the Architects themselves. Who are we as mere servants to their greatness to decide if one should be forgiven or not?'

'Forgiven or not.'

'May I be on my way, please?' Cregg asked carefully. The wrong words could keep him there until the moon rose the next day.

'You may be on your way. However, be mindful that we have now seen that child with you twice this day. A curious thing. A very curious thing, indeed. Be careful as you go now. May the Architects watch over you, always.'

'Over you, always.'

The Tal Valar always framed their thoughts through the lessons of the Architects, as if that instilled greater fear amongst the population. Cregg had always found it an odd curiosity that law and religion were blended together in this way. He felt there was more to them, often conducting their business behind a veil of mystery. They held daily preachings outside their many prayer lodges across the city and beyond, though only the Tal Valar themselves were allowed inside them unless formally invited in advance.

How one became a Tal Valar was unknown, too. Though, they always moved in pairs, and the senior of the two always had a finger missing on their right hand. Cregg often thought about that missing finger, as well as many other things about the mysterious defenders of the law in Moranza.

After a moment of silence between the three of them, the Tal Valar bowed and moved on their way, seemingly unbothered by Milo evading arrest. Cregg knew other members of the Tal Valar would be looking for the lad, too. He wondered how they communicated with each other. No one ever saw more than two together at any one time, yet communication occurred somehow. Perhaps it was telepathy. Some form of written communication was more likely. Maybe the Architects themselves worked amongst them, unseen by everyone else. Was there an Architect of Messages? Cregg shrugged to himself as he pondered the question, resuming his journey into the city. There was—so the Tal Valar say—an Architect for everything. Cregg could only remember a handful of them.

Milo was hiding in the shadows of the Moonwatch Tower in a small alcove often frequented by the less fortunate of society. The tower itself sat plum centre of the city square—a very circular square—with enough space for public events, like funerals and executions. Not that there had been any public executions in nearly fifty years. The palace, and by extension, the Tal Valar, projected a view of modern enlightenment, and that taking the life of a criminal was little better than murder in and of itself. What seems to have been forgotten by almost everyone is the year of riots that sprang from the execution of a young woman who was later proven to be innocent. Cregg had lived through those riots. They started soon after he took the position of Timekeeper and watched it all from the safety of the bell chamber above.

'Is it safe?' asked Milo, who looked pleased to see it was indeed Cregg who approached him.

'Yes, though I think it best we avoid any further encounters with the Tal Valar today.' He checked the moon's position. Time was running out. 'Right, let's get this over and done with.

Milo nodded eagerly as he stood and followed Cregg through the city. There were so many people now, all ready for the celebrations that would begin the moment the bell chimed. It was easy to get lost in the crowd. Everyone was in high spirits, each and every one of them wishing the pair a happy Last Moon as they jostled their way through the market and to the store.

'Well,' said Cregg as he put his hand on the door handle. 'Let's hope he's true to his word.'

Milo didn't reply.

8

The man Milo called Werral appeared from the back room as soon as they entered. His eyebrows were furrowed together as if becoming one, and his nostrils flared as he breathed. 'Now, there was me thinking yer had stolen me property,' he growled.

'I object to the accusation. You demanded a price for the lad, and I agreed to that price.' Cregg tried to keep his voice steady, hiding the fear scratching away at him from the inside.

'You have the egg?'

'I do.' Cregg fumbled in his pocket, catching the burnt skin on the back of his hand on the fabric. He grimaced through the pain, retrieved the egg and held it out, resting it in the centre of his palm.

'Very good. The question is, though, how would someone such as yer good self know where to find a dragon egg? And furthermore, once yer have found said egg, have the ability to procure it without... dying.'

'I have to admit, I did have some help from the lad,' said

Cregg. He indicated to Milo with a nod. Milo was lurking to his right, watching the exchange between his current master and his prospective new one.

'Is that so?' Werral glared at Milo before gesturing at Cregg to hand over the egg.

Cregg stepped forward, hand still aloft, and allowed the man to snatch the prize in his own greedy, grubby fingers. Werral turned it over in his own hand, his lip curling upwards a little.

'You'll release the lad into my custody, then,' said Cregg, trying to not make it sound like a question.

'Now, why would I do that?' snarled Werral.

Cregg jerked his head back in surprise, his eyes wider. That wasn't the answer he expected. He glanced at Milo, who had dropped his shoulders, as if expecting this outcome. 'It's what we agreed. One dragon egg for the boy.'

'Well, now that is where yer wrong. The agreement was for *yer* to bring me an egg before moonset in exchange for the boy. Yer didn't bring me an egg.'

'Yes, I did. I just gave it to you,' he insisted, jabbing a finger.

'No. *He* got the egg for yer. Without him, there would be no egg. The agreement is void.'

Werral made to step away, retreating into the back room. Cregg crossed the floor and pulled him by the shoulder. The man reacted by spinning, arm raised, and striking Cregg across the cheek with the back of his hand.

Milo rushed forward to intervene, but was rewarded with a strike around the back of the head for his efforts.

'This isn't right,' shouted Cregg. 'We had an agreement. If you don't honour it, I will find the Tal Valar and have them deal with you.'

Werral laughed. A full belly laugh. 'Oh, please do! Bring me here the authorities and have the boy taken away. Sent to the slate mines for the rest of his rotten, miserable life.'

'Better than to live under the beatings you hand out to him.' Cregg rubbed his face, still stinging from his own experience of the man's violence.

'Please stop!' wailed Milo.

'Yer stay out of this,' shouted Werral, raising his hand, ready to hit the boy yet again.

'Please, there has to be some arrangement we can come to. I brought you an egg. It was I who risked my life to find it.' He had forgotten *how* he found the egg, though deep down, something told him he spoke the truth. 'Yes, Milo showed me where to find it, but I was the one who took it, brought it to you. Surely that egg is worth more than enough to cover the life of one slave?

'Ha! Maybe it is, maybe it ain't. The boy's not fer sale. He never was. He should never have gone with yer.' He glared at Milo. 'Needs reminding of his place in the world, he does. We can't have slaves thinking they can come and go as they please. No. He will remain here with me, and I ask that yer leave. Yer business ain't welcome here. Go, forget about the boy.'

'We had an arrangement!' Cregg's skin prickled with heat, his heart racing. *How dare this man renege on the deal? Who does he think he is?*

'Get out!'

'Oh, I'm leaving, and I'm taking the lad with me.' He nodded at Milo, who looked utterly bewildered by the entire exchange, glancing alternately between the two. 'Come on, lad,' Cregg insisted. 'Choose your freedom.'

Cregg made for the door and Milo followed, his decision

made. Before he could open the door into the outside world wide enough to pass through, Werral had closed the distance between them. The man pulled at Cregg's shoulder, the long and dirty fingernails of his good arm digging into flesh through his shirt. Cregg grunted and fought to shake his assailant off, without success.

'Please! Stop!' cried Milo before receiving the back hand of his master, sending him to the floor.

What happened next was all a blur to Cregg. Somehow, he and Werral became entwined in a heap on the dirty floor, both wrestling for dominance. For freedom for the boy. He was too old for this, and the strength he once had was now a distant memory trapped in the past, along with a lifetime of regrets and missed opportunities.

For the merest of seconds, he thought he had the upper hand, landing a weak blow to Werral's cheek, the pain in his knuckles declaring at least one broken finger as payment. He howled, eyes closed, watering. And then it was over.

Pressure seized Cregg's throat. An artificial hand tightened around his windpipe, squeezing away however many years he had left in this world. Vision blurring, he couldn't breathe, couldn't think. He couldn't fight back any longer. *All this for a slave.*

And then the pressure released, air flooding back into his lungs as he gasped for life, to live on. *What happened?* He coughed and wheezed as his aching muscles fought Werral away. A wail and a grunt echoed around the room. Milo had come to his rescue, hitting the man repeatedly with what looked like an umbrella.

'I will kill yer both!' Werral declared, his good arm raised, defending the onslaught bestowed upon him by the boy.

Milo wouldn't be any match for the man any longer than

a second or two, but it was enough to allow Cregg to get to his feet. He pulled the door open and staggered into the street, the lad in tow. Such was their entrance into the world, anyone in the vicinity stopped to see what caused the commotion.

'Thief!' shouted Werral from behind—barely behind. 'That man has stolen my property!'

Cregg struggled to find a path through the crowd, who instinctively rounded on them upon hearing the man's cries. 'I've stolen nothing,' he shouted through heavy breaths to anyone who would listen. 'We had an agreement. I have freed his slave for honest payment.'

'Lies! Someone summon the Tal Valar! I want this man arrested at once!' The man lunged at Milo, attempting to grab him by the arm, but barely touching a finger to his sleeve.

'It's true. It's all true what this man says,' called Milo, pointing at Cregg. 'He has bought my freedom.'

The crowd watched on through gasps, grumbles, and confusion as the scene played out in front of them. Werral continued to call for the Tal Valar, but for once, none were present, or even imminent in their arrival. As much as there was confusion, the gathered audience prevented their escape. Cregg and Milo were trapped. A wall of bewildered onlookers behind, and a seething slave master with the potential for murder in front.

In a moment of madness, and a clarity only a lifetime of experience could provide, Cregg took Milo by the hand and demanded the boy followed his lead. With his good shoulder forward, and the skinny lad behind, he charged at Werral with everything he could muster, and bowled him clear of the door. Once inside, he slammed the door closed and bolted it, leaving Werral bellowing like a demon possessed on the other side.

Cregg allowed himself to slide down the door until he was sitting on the floor with his back to it, the door itself vibrating with repeated impacts from Werral trying to force it open from the outside.

'This ain't good. This ain't good at all,' said Milo as he paced back and forth through the extensive clutter around him.

'No, you're right, it's not. It was our only option, though what we do now, I don't know.'

'He will kill ya. When he gets inside, he will kill us both now, I think.'

Cregg contemplated the lad's words. He was right, and he should be terrified. Strangely, he felt a sense of calm, of resignation. Werral wasn't important. His concern was ensuring the bell rang on time. *How much time is left, though?* Not enough. Not nearly enough to escape from this predicament, preferably with the lad, and get to the top of the tower before the moon turned in for another day.

As he sat there, his back against the noise of plated metal being hammered at, he wondered what would happen if he *didn't* ring the bell. Everyone would notice, that's for sure, but beyond that? No one would be hurt. No one would die, most likely. The moon would still rise the following morning, and the city would continue on. It made him feel... inconsequential.

The hammering and shouting outside stopped.

'Help me to my feet, would you?' *This is becoming a habit.*

'Ya shouldn't have shut him out,' said Milo, pulling hard on Cregg's hand.

Back on his feet, he turned the handle of the door, ready

to peek outside to see if Werral really had gone and they could make their escape. It wouldn't turn. He tried again with more force, but the mechanism had jammed somehow, most likely by all the kicking and banging from the other side.

'Is there another way out of here?'

'Yes, of course. We have a back door. Everyone has a back door.'

'The tower doesn't have one.'

Milo shook his head. 'This way. We have to be quick.' He led the way through the dirty curtain that separated the public shop from the private quarters.

The back area was more filthy and chaotic than the front. By modest opinion, the shop was practically pristine compared to the mess out the back. The floor and every surface, every shelf and nook, were covered with every conceivable item possible. Broken things, once discarded, now hoarded here in the hope they might once again be needed. All of it junk, all of it worthless. And all of it stank. Cregg did his best to breathe through his mouth, gagging as he danced through all the mess on the floor, doing his best not to get any on his shoes.

'How can you live like this?' he asked.

'Ya get used to it. He makes me clean it, but he makes the mess faster than I can fix it. Blames me for it all, of course.'

'Of course.'

At the back of the mess was another door. Tatty, worn and missing its plate on the top half. It had been painted, once, perhaps a shade of blue, but it was hard to tell given the state of it.

'Where do you sleep?'

Milo pointed to a heap of dirty rags in the opposite

corner. Cregg wanted to feel sorry for the lad, but there wasn't any time for that. He knew in that moment that he *was* doing the right thing, and if they could escape this place, Milo would have a better life in the tower. He would have to plead his case to the Tal Valar, and persuade them there indeed was a valid contract for Milo's release, and remove the metal band from his wrist. And hopefully, have any charges against the lad dropped.

There would be time for all that, though. *One thing at a time.* Before either of them reached the door, it exploded inwards, coming clear off its hinges except for a small part at the bottom. Cregg recoiled from the flying fragments of door, covering his face with his arm.

'Nice try.' Werral, angrier than ever, blocked the way out to freedom. Cregg and Milo were trapped. 'Let me show yer how thieves are treated here.'

'I'm not a thief. You changed the deal,' stammered Cregg, inching backwards.

'I said, *yer* bring me an egg. Not the boy. He belongs to me, so anything he finds or steals already belongs to me by right of the law.'

Strictly speaking, the man was correct, but in Cregg's mind it was only semantics. He'd done as asked, and it *was* he who took the egg, he was sure of that. Although, if Milo hadn't shown him the way, he'd have nothing. *Am I really in the wrong here?* Self-doubt ate away at his thoughts as he tried to think of a way to calm Werral down quickly, before someone got hurt. Or worse.

'Surely we can come to a new arrangement? I can find you a second egg tomorrow. Two eggs for the lad's life. That has to be a great deal for you.'

'The boy ain't fer sale. And then there's the damages.

They need paying for, too.' Werral cracked the knuckles of his good hand with the artificial one, grinning through uncared-for teeth.

'Damages? What damages?'

'Do yer see me door?'

'*You* broke that!'

'Maybe I did, maybe I didn't. Yer fault though. Locking me out of me own shop like that. No choice in the matter.'

Cregg looked to Milo in the hope he'd say something or *do* something to alleviate the situation. Unfortunately, the lad looked absolutely petrified and had shrunk away into a corner, making himself look as small as possible. Cregg had to think fast, come up with a solution—one that would get him and Milo out from this Architects-damned shop and back to the tower.

Had he been twenty years younger, he might have found himself emboldened enough to try taking the man on in a straight fight. Today? There was no chance of him winning, even if he hadn't been bruised and battered by the events that brought it all to this. And even with Werral missing an arm, he doubted the advantage of that, too.

'No point looking at that worthless scrap. He won't help yer.'

'If he's so worthless to you, let him go.'

'Nah.'

What Cregg needed right now was some sort of distraction. Some way of getting the man away from the door so he could make his escape and pray to the Architects the lad had · the wherewithal to follow. He glanced around at the mess of the storeroom. Six paces to his left was a very cheap, very old shelving unit, overstuffed with who-knows-what in the way of unsaleable good. If he could...

He darted—ankle be damned—to the shelves and pushed. 'If I can't have the lad, I'll destroy everything. It won't only be the door you'll have to replace!'

At first, the shelves didn't budge, proving far sturdier than they appeared. Eventually, they gave way in a cascade of items crashing to the floor around him, kicking up dust and flecks of... he didn't want to know what. Werral reacted as Cregg had hoped—dashing forward from the doorway in his direction. The contents of the shelves were not on the man's mind—no, he was charging right for Cregg, scrambling across the room while throwing any obstacle out of the way that dared to block his path.

'I will end yer,' growled the man. 'Who do yer think yer are?'

'I am the official timekeeper of this city and I am taking the lad as agreed. The Tal Valar will side with me, you'll see. It is time for us to leave, and time is of the essence. I bid you good day, sir!' Cregg had already decided which way he would run when faced with the inevitable attack. Despite his age, he dodged Werral's grasp, hopped over a box that had spilled its contents—much to the complaints of his knees and ankle—and made a break for the door.

Milo wasn't so lucky. He had followed Cregg's lead and made for the exit, but somehow, Werral had seized him by the leg, causing the lad to lose his balance and land chest first on some dubious-looking meat.

'Get ya hand off me!' Milo screamed. The panic in his voice echoed around the room.

Cregg stopped short of the door and looked back as Milo kicked and writhed, trying his best to escape the clutches of his now former master. He could make his escape, leaving the lad behind, then try to find the nearest pair of Tal Valar and beg for their intervention. Milo's visible injuries should be enough to convince them the lad would be better off away from that awful man. But he was still a slave. All the while he wore that bracelet, he was still the property of his owner, and the law didn't extend as far as the well-being of slaves any more than they did the care of cooking utensils. Nobody got arrested for breaking a pot, and to his knowledge, no one got arrested for beating a slave.

No—it was all down to him. If he was to save the lad from this cruel and horrific man, it would be up to him, and only him. How, though?

To his right, amongst the grime and debris of the shattered door, lay a length of metal piping. Without a second thought, Cregg snatched the pipe with his good hand. It was heavy enough to cause some damage. Within seconds, and without fully thinking his actions through, he closed the distance between them and slammed the piping—rust and all—into Werral's back. The man screamed in a mixture of surprise and agony, his grasp releasing Milo.

Werral was hurt, but not stopped. Cregg swung a second time, but the advantage of surprise was lost, and he missed. He hesitated, and that was enough time to allow the man to make him his target and retaliate with a punch to the stomach, taking all the air from his lungs with a groan.

Milo didn't choose to escape, coming instead to Cregg's aid in much the same way he'd done for him. Two against one, all fighting for dominance, for survival. For freedom.

Somewhere in the fracas, Cregg had sliced his arm on something sharp. He didn't see what, only the blood running down his arm, covering anything he touched. He was losing this fight. *They* were losing this fight. He was too old, and Milo was too small and weak against this ugly mess of a man. Thanks to a distraction from Milo, Cregg managed to get to his feet, unsteady in his balance.

Werral had his back to him, his attention on Milo, who was trying his best to keep any obstacle between them. All breathing heavily, exhausted and bruised, they stood in a stand-off. Werral in the middle, Cregg behind. All eyes on Milo.

Something had changed, though. Milo's hands were glowing, a soft white light in each palm. From where Cregg stood, the lad didn't seem to have noticed. Werral definitely knew something was wrong, not that Cregg could see the expression on his face. It was a shift in his body language that gave him away.

'Let us go,' said Milo softly.

'I'd sooner kill yer. Kill yer both.'

Cregg inched forward, silently creeping up on the man. If he could get his arm around Werral's neck and squeeze with all the strength he had left, then maybe—just maybe—he could choke him enough that he passed out. The idea of killing a man outright still didn't sit right with him, even now. If everyone came out of this alive, so much the better.

Cregg's foot caught on something unseen on the floor, alerting Werral to the threat behind him. He spun before Cregg was anywhere near close enough to reach. Cregg swallowed. There were no other options left now. It was over. He winced as the man raised his fist, ready to receive the blow that would finish him. An image of Petral appeared in his mind as he contemplated the end. *I'm sorry.* He inhaled fast as Werral's fist came at him.

9

The anticipated punch to the face never came. There was only a strange groan from Werral before he doubled over and collapsed to the floor. His eyes were wide open, but the life within them had gone. He lay there—motionless—with his real arm tucked into his chest as if bound to his heart.

'Huh? What happened?' Cregg asked, his own heart still racing.

'I think I killed him,' said Milo, in barely more than a whisper. His hands were no longer glowing. There was a sadness in his eyes.

'What do you mean, killed him? What did you do?' He knelt beside Werral and checked for signs of life. Nothing. There wasn't any blood, not as far as he could see through the mess around them. No sign of injury either, nor any weapon.

'I killed him with my magic. I don't know how. It just... happened. I pushed him away with my mind, and it just... happened. He fell, and he died.'

From outside came shouting. No, Cregg decided, not shouting. Calling. Someone was coming their way. Someone else would soon witness the disarray around them and discover the dead man on the floor. Beside Werral's body lay the egg, undamaged and distinct from all the other detritus scattered around. He quickly pocketed it, hidden from whoever approached. A few seconds later, the figures of two Tal Valar brothers entered via the broken door.

'Say nothing,' Cregg whispered to Milo. 'Follow my lead.'

'By the Architects themselves! What event has occurred here this day?'

'Here this day.'

Cregg didn't recognise the pair. Thankfully, they weren't the ones he'd already seen twice today, though he doubted they wouldn't already know more than any normal man should. This time, the one with the missing finger—the one who did most of the talking, and indicating seniority—was the shorter of the two. The second was at least a head taller, and his robe poorly hid a strong, muscular frame. Neither had shaved heads. Most preferred to be bald, though not all. Cregg often wondered if there was a reason behind that too, along with the missing fingers.

'A pleasant Last Moon to you both.' Cregg bowed respectfully as he spoke. 'I was conducting business with this fellow—a good, long-standing friend of mine—and he was taken rather ill.' He looked to Milo. 'Isn't that right?'

Milo nodded tentatively, unsure, hiding guilt.

'Does he require assistance?' asked the brother.

'Require assistance.'

'I'm sorry to say he's quite dead. There was nothing I could do for him. It happened so fast. We were negotiating a price when he suddenly grabbed his chest and dropped dead on the spot. If I were to guess, and I am no surgeon, of course, I would say it was his heart. May the Architects look after his soul, and may Aelene herself guide him to the next life.'

'May the Architects keep him,' said the brother with a raised eyebrow as he attention turned to the destruction around them.

'Keep him.'

Cregg lowered his head as a mark of respect, pretending not to notice the brothers' curiosity. He was sweating, but there was nothing he could do about that.

'Are you certain of this? One might argue there has been some sort of altercation. We were summoned here by a market trader who spoke of an argument.'

'Of an argument.'

'Nothing to do with us, I can assure you,' said Cregg as he scratched his neck. 'Regrettably, I find myself rather pressed for time. I need to get back to the tower to ring the bell for moonset. So, I bid you good day, and will leave you to take care of the necessary arrangements here.'

Cregg stepped forward to pass the two men, but the short one held out his arm to stop him. The brother eyed Milo with the same concern as the corpse on the floor. 'Is this the matter of the affair, child? May the Architects guide you to offer forth the truth, and only the truth.'

'Only the truth.'

'Y-yes,' Milo stammered. 'He complained of pains all day. Then just now he grabbed his chest as if he'd been stabbed by an invisible knife and down he fell. He reached for the shelf there, see.' He pointed to the mess.

'And what of the door?'

'Of the door.'

Milo looked to Cregg for an answer, but he equally could not come up with a plausible explanation.

'I'm sorry, I have no idea,' Cregg said. 'Now, if you would please excuse me. I really have to go.'

Before the two Tal Valar could say anything more, Cregg made a run for it, gesturing with his hand for Milo to follow. He had no intention of staying in this awful place any longer and certainly wasn't in any mind for another fight. He *had* to get to the tower and ring the bell. That was all that mattered —if he wasn't already too late. He was sure he wasn't. Even in all that had happened, he would have noticed the dimming sky of twilight through the window, or what little was left of the door.

The two robed figures gave chase immediately, both calling for them to stop. Of course they did. Anyone with half an imagination would think there had been a murder, and that either he or the boy—or both—were responsible. None of was important right now.

Cregg pushed his way through the mass of people in the market, hoping to lose himself among them. Somewhere deep in the middle, shortly after he accidentally knocked a young woman off her feet because she didn't see him in time, he lost sight of the Tal Valar behind him. He'd lost Milo too. One moment he was right behind him, the next he was gone. Cregg couldn't move fast, and his old bones made his movements cumbersome, yet still he found himself on his own, fleeing the cloaked arm of the law. He couldn't risk stopping, waiting for the lad to find him, or catch up with him.

The moon, what would be left of it at this time of day, was hidden somewhere behind the city buildings. The normal orange of the sky now had a slight tinge of purple to it, its own warning twilight was imminent.

By the time he reached the door of the tower, he was ready to collapse with exhaustion. He leaned on the wall by the door with one hand, head down, panting. *One hundred and eighty-seven.* The number that stood between him and the bell. The number of steps he had to climb, probably faster than he'd ever had to climb them. He glanced back to where he came. No sign of Milo, and no sign of the Tal Valar, either. Maybe the Architects were on his side. After all, he had tried to do the right thing by the lad.

They would find him, though. He knew that.

Sucking in as much air as he could, forcing back a cough from the dry dust entering his lungs, Cregg entered the tower and climbed.

Every step was more laboured than the last. His legs felt as though they were becoming stone themselves. Inside his chest, his heart thumped away angrily, protesting at the strain it and the rest of his body was forced to endure. He gritted his teeth and pushed on. *Thirty. Forty.* He allowed himself to stop at sixty-four, the step underneath the only window along the way up the tower. It offered a good view of the square, and the closest edge of the market. Two cloaked figures were running toward the tower. *The same ones?* It mattered not. Still no sign of Milo. If the Tal Valar were running for the tower, Milo had likely gone to ground.

'Stay hidden, lad. I'll put this right, I promise. One last ring of the bell, then I'll put this right.'

He pushed onwards. Upwards. One step at a time, as best as he could muster, unsure if he had the strength left to reach the top. By the hundredth step, the sound of voices far below climbed the spiralled walls around him. They were coming. He was more than halfway there, but they would be faster. A race against time was now also a race with the law. With the Tal Valar. With freedom, and the Architects who oversaw it all.

The black eyes of the secret dragon greeted him as he pulled himself up on hands and knees over the final step. 'Hello, my little friend,' he said, wheezing. He'd made it. As he staggered past the bell to retrieve his hammer, the last vestiges of the moon slid below the horizon, darkening the sky. He was late, but only by mere seconds. *No one will notice.*

Hammer tight in his grasp, he swung hard and true. The bell sang out its one note tune. Far below, the city cheered— a sound that rippled outward from the square, carried on the breeze. A new year had begun, and it was time for the world to celebrate. For everyone except him, at least.

Exhausted, he let the hammer fall from his hand and he smiled at the dragon. The creature eyed him. It looked... angry.

'Hey, what's the matter, little one? Are you hungry? I'm sorry, it's been quite a day.' He moved closer to the dragon, offering a hand. It reacted aggressively, its only wing outstretched and flapping. It shrieked and tried to spit at him, though no liquid came from its mouth. Cregg furrowed his brow and withdrew his hand. Not once had he seen the dragon react in this manner.

He remembered he still had the egg in his pocket. Maybe it could sense it through his clothing. He retrieved it and showed it to the dragon, hoping it might appease it in some way. It only made the creature more angry. It screamed and snapped its jaws at him from its hollow perch within the tower wall, demonstrating a fury that needed no words.

The two Tal Valar chose that moment to appear at the

top of the steps. It was indeed the two who had stumbled upon him, Milo, and the dead body of Werral.

'You are required to come with us to answer for the charge of murder,' said the senior brother.

'Charge of murder.'

'I will come peacefully. My task here is done. However, I stand by my word and that I had no hand in the man's death. Nor did the lad.'

'Whether your words hold the truth, you will be judged by the Architects themselves, and they alone will decide. You must come with—'

The dragon cried out from its alcove, interrupting the brother. Even the second one didn't offer any words of repetition. All eyes turned to the gap in the wall.

'In the name of the Architects!' gasped the senior brother. 'It is not permitted to have a dragon in your possession! Is there no end to your crime?'

'To your crime.'

'It is old and injured,' protested Cregg. He instinctively moved to put himself between the Tal Valar and the dragon, but the animal only grew more agitated. Cregg inched away a little. 'It made its own way here. It cannot fly, and is safe from everyone up here. There isn't any danger, I assure you.'

The dragon continued screaming at the three of them, washing away any true belief in Cregg's words.

'Dragons are always dangerous wherever they are found.'

'They are found.'

The taller, junior Tal Valar produced a small cloth bag from within his robes and attempted to secure the dragon, only to have the creature bite his finger, drawing blood. The man yelped in surprise—the first words Cregg had witnessed the man speak of his own, being the very worst of profanity unbecoming of a Tal Valar brother.

Before the man could make a second attempt, another dragon settled on the open wall beside them. This one had brilliant red scales, strong, winged forearms, and sharp claws that clicked ominously against the stonework.

'There is never but only one!'

'Only one!'

The two brothers backed away from the wall towards the steps, aghast and mouths open. For his part, Cregg moved away from the two dragons and away from the steps.

Three more dragons arrived, all angry and vocal, their attentions directed at Cregg. 'I think they want this,' he said, holding up the egg. Immediately, the dragons reacted. One of the tiny beasts on the wall launched itself at Cregg, attempting to snatch the egg. It missed, and continued past his ear so close he could feel the air move beneath the dragon's wing.

He tried desperately to wave the dragons away as they began attacking him. More and more of the flying creatures arrived by the second, until there were too many to count. The two Tal Valar escaped down the steps, leaving Cregg to fend off the dragons by himself.

'Take it!' he screamed, tossing the egg at the dragons. 'I don't want it! I never wanted it!'

The swarm of dragons didn't listen. Whether or not they wanted the egg, he couldn't see, as he got lost within a sea of red against the darkened sky. Together as one, they attacked him. As he tried to evade the onslaught, his heel caught on something. His hammer, still where he'd dropped it in his exhaustion only moments before.

He lost his balance, forcing him back until he had

nowhere else to go. His whole bodyweight pressed against the wall of the tower... until it wasn't. The section of stonework he'd been pleading to have fixed for years gave out on him, and it supported him no longer.

As he fell from the tower, surrounded by the dragons escorting his descent in a maelstrom of primal predation, he saw his wife. He saw everything, his whole life, from his earliest memory through to his last. He saw his parents, and he saw Petral. Oh, how beautiful she had been. How beautiful she always was to him all throughout their years together. His sons. One last time he saw them, recalling the good times before he lost them, too. And finally, Milo, the boy he met mere hours ago. In his final second of life, he wished the lad the best of lives now he was free of that despicable man.

IO

The dark purple of the fleeting twilight sky faded into its usual orange as Cregg opened his eyes. He blinked rapidly as he watched the distant shapes of dragons circling the top of the tower as it loomed over him, his back to the ground. 'I really thought I was going to die,' he said, mostly to himself as he realised he felt no pain.

'And you would be correct,' said a voice, out of his eye-line behind him. A woman's voice, though not one he was familiar with.

Cregg craned his neck to see. There was someone standing over him. In fact, there were *many* people standing over him. They all wore an expression of shock, or sorrow. Some covered their mouths with their hands, tears wetting their cheeks. Except one. Something about her felt out of place compared to the rest of them.

He pushed himself onto his elbows and swivelled to get a better look at the woman. She was tall, with a slender frame. In her fifties, if he had to guess. A thin pair of spectacles rested on a narrow nose. Her hair was a mix of dark blonde and grey. To him, she looked beautiful. In contrast to the usual drab brown and grey attire worn by most inhabitants of the city, this woman wore a dress of pure white, save for some simple black embellishments around the shoulders and sleeves.

'I'm sorry,' said Cregg. 'Do I know you?'

'I am sure you know *of* me. Though, you will not have had cause to meet me until today.' The woman offered a half-smile through her spectacles as she stared down at him.

'No, I can't say that I do. Why are all these other people here?' He looked around at the dozen or so others. 'What's the matter? Have I done something?'

'You have learned the lesson that a man cannot fly,' she replied.

'Well, I know *that*.'

'Take a good look around you. A proper look. Then you will understand.'

He cocked an eyebrow at her, then looked around him. More people were gathering around him, one by one, all watching with... what *was* that look? Pity? The dragons still circled the top of the tower. He had been among them only moments ago. He didn't remember coming back down the steps. No, the Tal Valar brothers had escaped the attack, leaving him all alone.

And then he realised. He remembered. 'I fell, didn't I?'

'In a manner of speaking,' said the woman.

'How did I survive that? I'm not even injured.' He looked for the burn on his hand, but there was nothing there, as if it had never happened.

'That is why I am here. You did not survive.' She tutted. 'Honestly, you do seem a little slow. *Look.*'

He scrambled to his feet, stepping away. The woman

wasn't as tall as he'd first assumed. In fact, she was barely an inch taller than him. She locked eyes with him, then nodded once to the spot where he'd lain.

There, on the ground, surrounded by so many onlookers, he saw himself. A crumpled mess, broken by the forces of nature that kept everything that couldn't fly tethered to the dirt. Blood pooled underneath his head. The dead version of himself's eyes were still open, though they no longer saw.

He gasped, eyes widened. 'If I'm dead, and you're speaking to me, then that means you're...'

'Yes, my name is Aelene, and you are as dead as anyone could hope for.'

'The Architect of *Death*.'

'Dear, do not say it like that. It makes it sound like I was the cause of,' she circled a finger over his corpse, 'this mess.'

'Yes, of course,' he replied, humbled.

'Now the introductions are over, it is time for us to leave. Come along now. You are not the only one to die today. So many others are waiting. In fact,' she cocked her head. 'A bridge has collapsed not far from here. Twenty people all dead at once. No... make that twenty-one. Oh dear, oh dear. Such a sad fate for them all.'

'I can't go. Not yet.'

Aelene sighed impatiently. 'Dear, no one is ever ready for me. So much more you all want to do, as if you wish to live forever. And that just will not do. It is your time.'

'No. I must know about the lad. I need to know he's safe. I promised him.'

'It is too late for that. Your time in this world is at an end. I am here to escort you safely to the next life.'

He ignored her and tried to push his way through the crowd. It surprised him when they didn't move out of the way, and he simply passed through them as if they were nothing. Except it was he who was nothing. He no longer had a body. *Am I only a soul now?* He stumbled as he passed through the body of a Tal Valar brother who had arrived to disperse the crowd and see for himself what incident had taken place. Silent, his companion speaking on behalf of them both, save for the last few words, as always.

'You must come with me,' insisted Aelene, her tone a mixture of boredom and indignation. 'Why must it be so hard for you humans to accept death when she comes?'

'Not until I find him,' Cregg replied. He didn't have to go far, in fact. Milo was by the side of the tower, back to the wall and feet tucked up to his chest. *Did he watch me fall?* Cregg went to crouch beside him.

'I was supposed to save him.'

'Were you? Why?'

'She told me to do the right thing.'

'She? Ah, an intervention of fate. Yes, I understand what you mean. Did you ever consider that your paths crossed so he could save you, too?'

Cregg furrowed his brow and looked at the god looming over him. 'Why would I need saving?'

'You have lived more in this one day than you have in the last ten, no? Merely existing, waiting for the end. The child changed all that. For one final day, you were truly *alive*, and now is the time to rest.'

'I need to say goodbye.'

'He cannot see you,' Aelene said. She stood beside him, imposing.

'He might,' Cregg whispered. 'Lad, I'm sorry. It's time for me to go now. You're free to be the person you always dreamed of being. Oh, how I wish I was young again, with my whole life in front of me. You have no idea how lucky you are.'

Milo didn't react. He wasn't even looking Cregg's way.

The lad stared into the air, his arm resting on his knee, idly playing with the copper bracelet on his wrist that told everyone he was still a slave, even if he had no longer had a master.

Cregg lowered his head in shame when he saw it. 'I should have removed it when I had the chance.' *Did I have the chance? Everything happened so fast!* 'If only I could remove it for you now.' He reached out to touch the metal band, knowing he could not.

Except.

As his fingers passed without resistance through the bracelet, it split in two and fell to the ground with a clatter. Milo started, the sound breaking him from his daydream.

'Did I do that?' Cregg asked of Aelene.

'No, I think not. I wonder if he was touched by the Origem itself at one time. The boy has potential within him. I can see it, and I can see why fate brought you together.'

Cregg didn't know that word. *Origem*. Somehow it resonated deep inside whatever was left of him. He asked Aelene what it meant, but she only responded with a wry smile.

Milo rubbed at his wrist as he realised what had happened and what it meant for him. His face lit up, beaming, and then he saw Cregg in front of him. Or at least, that's what Cregg believed, as the boy was looking right where he was kneeling.

'Be free now, Milo. Be free,' Cregg said.

'I'll never forget you,' said Milo, grinning. 'Never. I promise.' He pulled himself to his feet and skipped away without glancing back.

'He saw me,' declared Cregg. 'He saw me, didn't he?'

'If that is what you wish to believe. It is not my place to deny you. I am only here to—'

'Yeah, yeah. Take me to the next life. I'm ready now, except... my life's work. Who will ring the bell? Who will keep time?' he asked, standing. For the first time in decades, his knees didn't complain.

'That is no longer your concern. Time will continue on, as it always has, and as it always will. And now is your time to move on.'

He sighed, resigned, and then he realised. 'Will Petral be there?'

'Petral? Ah yes, I remember her. Sweet woman. Though, as I recall, she was somewhat annoyed to see me, too.'

'Oh?'

'She was in the middle of cooking your dinner.'

AFTERWORD

Thank you for picking up this novella, I hope you enjoyed it! If you did, I invite you to continue your journey into the world I have created with the first full length novel *Orchestra of the Gods* which is available right now. Full details can be found on my website damien-buckley.com either follow the link or scan the QR code below to take you there.

Also, please may I encourage you to leave a review for this book wherever you prefer to leave them. They help more than you might realise!

BV - #0197 - 031125 - C0 - 198/129/6 - PB - 9781917700054 - Matt Lamination